CONNIE B. DOWELL

Airplanes and Alibis

To my sister Katie. May you soar high.

Contents

Chapter 1   1

Chapter 2   9

Chapter 3   14

Chapter 4   21

Chapter 5   28

Chapter 6   33

Chapter 7   42

Chapter 8   48

Chapter 9   53

Chapter 10   57

Chapter 11   69

Chapter 12   73

Chapter 13   76

Chapter 14   79

Chapter 15   84

Get a Free Story   88

Author's Note   91

About the Author   92

Also by Connie B. Dowell   93

Chapter 1

Emmie

The roar of an engine pierced the afternoon quiet. I dropped the novel I was holding on the desk, raced to my bedroom window, and pushed aside the lacy curtains. A dusty truck marked US MAIL idled on the street outside the house. My heart thumped. I bolted downstairs, my shoes banging against the steps.

I barely registered Granny looking up from her armchair in surprise and muttering, "Is there an elephant in the house?"

Momma was only just closing the door as I hurried into the entryway. She looked up in alarm, a stack of letters clutched in her hand.

"Is it—" I didn't get a chance to finish the question.

"Emmeline McAllister!" she shouted in a loud and shrill voice that made me flinch, the kind of lecturing voice that sometimes the neighbors could hear—and they'd tease me about it later. "Were you, a woman of nearly twenty years, rushing tornado-like through the whole house like a small child?"

I blinked. "Well, as you saw me do it, you know I was, but—"

She still wouldn't let me finish. "My goodness, one would think you'd been raised in a pig stye! What have I been doing all these years that you feel this is appropriate behavior?"

"I'm sorry, Momma. I'll try not to run, but—"

She interrupted again, wagging a finger. She'd hit her stride. "If you end up

1

going to the university, your professors and classmates are going to expect a certain level of decorum."

I eyed the envelopes in her hand. "Speaking of the university, there didn't happen to be any mail addressed to—"

"You aren't listening as usual." Momma sighed. "No, there's no mail for you today." She stepped past me.

My shoulders slumped. Only a year ago had women first been allowed to be admitted to The University of Georgia, but only as juniors. This spring was my and my dearest friend Dessa's last term at The Lucy Cobb Institute, where we were doing our first two years of college. We were currently back home on Easter break. We'd sent our applications to the university months ago. It was now April. Decisions would have to come out soon. My teachers at Lucy Cobb had promised to send along any response they received during the break. Maybe it would be in tomorrow's mail.

I shuffled into the kitchen to make a cup of tea. I didn't feel much like reading anymore. I set the kettle to boil and watched out the kitchen window while a robin hopped around the tree outside. *They're only taking so many women,* I told myself. *It's no slight on you if you aren't one of them. You can always try again.* But I knew I could only keep trying so long. I'd gone back and forth on whether I'd go to South Carolina if I didn't get into Georgia. But there was no acceptance letter from there yet, either.

On top of it all, I couldn't find any distraction in reading the newspaper, as it announced that yesterday Delaware had rejected the suffrage amendment. It would have been final state needed if it had ratified.

Granny waddled into the kitchen and patted me on the back with a silent smile that I returned as she took the whistling kettle from the stove. I'd always be good enough for her at least. Maybe. When I thought about everyone else... Dessa studied every moment of the day. Dessa studied for fun. She was sure to be among the chosen few. Hank, freshly back from France and with an excellent high school record, had naturally been admitted this past fall, when the campus finally reopened post-wartime. Me? I was the girl who always had to be told to sit up straighter, to stop talking in class, to not be so silly. That's what everyone thought I was. Silly. Frivolous.

But I wasn't. I wanted a degree. I wanted to it for me and I wanted it to show Momma and Granny who never had the chance to get that far. Did that sound so silly?

Granny nudged me in the arm. "Tea's ready darling. Come on. Let's take it into the parlor." So, we did. We sat facing the open window, breathing in the perfume of the blooming camellia bushes. "It's not so bad, is it?" she said. "Some other state will come through for us soon. And remember the air show is this weekend."

* * *

Dessa

I heard the mail truck sputter away. My heart jumped to my throat. I had to get there first.

I left the parlor as silently as I could manage, every step across the patterned rug a calculated risk. If the letter was there and I got it first, I could choose how to deliver the news. If my father got that letter or my mother, they would set the tone for the conversation. They might make up their mind before I'd had any chance to speak mine. I had to get to the mail first.

I tiptoed across the floor to the entryway, but Flossie, the maid, popped out of the library and crossed ahead of me. Flossie was new to us, and I still didn't know her really. We'd had maids in the past who had been sympathetic, slipping me mail from my former lover—ugh, that word, but there wasn't a better one; beau didn't work when the object of your interest was a girl—before my parents could see. We had always been so careful, coding our letters, saying very little, but they still might have seen through. It was safest for them not to see at all.

But Flossie, would she deliver my mail straight to me? Would she dare take that risk?

Flossie opened the door and pulled the envelopes from the letterbox. Turning back inside and shutting the door with a snap, she flashed me a smile. "Nothing for you today. Sorry."

I smiled and nodded back. Nothing today. But maybe tomorrow. How I wished I had stood up for myself. Insisted that my school hold any decision mail for me. But when the teachers had asked me if I wanted them to forward my decision letter over break like the other handful of girls applying, when they gave me such encouraging smiles, wondered aloud how proud my parents must be, how could I explain how it really was?

It would mean an argument whether or not I got in. But as long as Flossie gave my mail straight to me—and I now thought she might—if I was rejected, I could burn it and pretend nothing had happened at all, that my dreams weren't crashing all around me.

A knock at the door made me jump. I spun around and sprinted to the door before Flossie could react. I wrenched it open. Emmie stood on the step, bouncing on the balls of her feet. Behind her in the road sat her shiny green Harley-Davidson and sidecar.

"Did anything come for you?" she asked.

I shook my head.

She sighed. "Me neither. Do you want to go out to McPherson's? My granny says we should get out and do something to distract us." McPherson's farm was where the air show—what folks sometimes called a barnstormer—would be held that weekend. I supposed they were already starting celebrations.

"That sounds lovely," I said. I turned to face Flossie who was peering around a corner. "Could you tell my parents?"

She nodded. "I'll tell them where you went if they ask."

I nodded back and hurried to get a sweater from my room. *If they ask.* My parents vacillated between obsessively controlling what I did and who I saw and total neglect. I never knew which way the pendulum would swing, but Emmie was usually on the approved list of associates because her uncle was the sheriff, even if my parents didn't like her family's progressive politics.

I followed Emmie to the road and climbed in the sidecar. Emmie settled herself on the bike. She took a small pin box from her pocket and pinned her skirt in place. "Not riding in the trousers today?" I asked.

She shrugged. "They need washing. This'll do in a pinch." She gave a wry smile. "That's our whole lives isn't it? This'll do in a pinch?"

CHAPTER 1

We sped through our small hometown of Cora, Georgia, passing garden beds overflowing with tulips in red and yellow and lilies in every window box. Posters hung from nearly every lamppost, some of them advertising the air show "Barnstormer Bonanza with Hollywood's Ellis Singleton!" and others detailing Sunday's Easter egg hunt.

We soon left town and turned down winding, red, dirt roads through the rolling north Georgia hills until we pulled into McPherson's and parked the motorcycle in a field. I was surprised to see the field was fairly full of cars already. The fun really must be starting.

"Is Hank coming?" I asked as I climbed out of the sidecar. Hank was Emmie's beau who had been a pilot during the war and was currently home from the university on Easter holidays.

"He's already here," Emmie replied, climbing off the bike and unpinning her skirt. "One of his pilot friends is doing stunt flying this weekend and he wanted to chat with him before the show really got started. Maybe we can meet him, too."

I would have expected Emmie to say "Maybe we can sit in the plane" or to joke about doing some wing walking. Her voice was flatter than usual. She was worried about college, too. I put a hand on her arm.

"I'm sure it'll be fine," I said, "no matter what happens."

She didn't have to ask what I was talking about. "I don't know. I'm..." her shoulders slumped. "They aren't taking many women, and I'm not good enough."

I frowned at her. "Of course, you're good enough. You finished the high school curriculum a whole year ahead of schedule. And we don't know anything for certain until the letters come."

"I suppose," Emmie replied. "And if I don't get into Georgia, maybe I will get into one of the other schools I applied to. Momma and Granny couldn't be too disappointed."

I felt the color drain out of my face. Emmie's eyebrows raised in alarm. "You did apply to other schools too, right?"

I shook my head. "It was risky enough applying to Georgia. I still don't know what I'll do if I get in. Or even if I don't get in."

5

Emmie bit her lip and ran one hand through her hair, ruffling it from its pins. "This is all so out of our control. We need to do something to take control back. If we can't do anything more to influence whether we get in and we don't know how long we'll be stuck waiting, let's make a contingency plan. If we decide what we're going to do with our lives if we don't get into college, then whatever happens we will be ready."

I pulled on my cardigan and hugged it tightly around me. A plan. Even if it wasn't the plan that I wanted. I could live with that. "I guess I have to figure out how to escape." I had long since decided there was no way I would stay under my parents' roof after I graduated Lucy Cobb. I'd had to get rid of two potential husbands already. Every time one of my parents visited the school, they would walk pointedly toward the window where so many girls had carved their initials with their new diamond engagement rings. My parents never said a word, just looked at the window and then at me, but the message was clear.

"You can always come live with my family."

I smiled. Her family had always been so kind to me.

I had thought Emmie was done speaking, but suddenly she added, "You're the daughter Momma wishes she had anyway."

"That's not true," I objected, but she gave a sad smile. "Besides," I said, "my parents wouldn't let me live away from them in the same town. They'd—" My mind ran over and over the possibilities. Ship me off to a sanitarium? Who knew what they might do in retaliation? No. The way was to go somewhere they couldn't find me.

She wrinkled her nose side to side in the way that meant she was thinking hard. "Have you got any money of your own?"

"I'm afraid not. Not that I can touch anyway. I'm honestly not sure what I'd do about tuition if I do get into the university. My grandfather left me some money, I'm not sure exactly how much. But it's for when I get married, not really for me at all."

Emmie nodded, her mouth set. "That's it, then. We have to figure out how to get you that money."

"I don't know how that's going to happen." We walked away from the cars and toward the festivities.

"We'll find a way. Then you can get set up someplace. Find yourself a job. Reapply to college next year if you want."

A job? "If I can't get into college and become a doctor, maybe I could try training as a nurse. Or some sort of medical assistant."

Emmie snorted. "Honestly, I cannot imagine you not getting into college. Even if you didn't get into Georgia this year, you'd be sure to get in somewhere else next year. I mean, what do you have in your pockets right now?" She looked sideways at me.

I stuck both hands in my pockets and felt around. "Some loose change?"

"And?"

"And..." My right hand ran over the smooth surface of my pocket notebook. Just some notes. And I guess a pencil, too."

"What notes?"

I squirmed. "Anatomy." I couldn't help it. Ever since the previous summer when we had been wrapped up in yet another murder mystery and I had actually gotten to speak to a medical examiner, I had been fascinated the intricacies of these amazing strange bodies all our souls live in. To think that with the right knowledge you could rescue someone from death, determine how someone died, or discover something about how we all tick and keep more people from suffering!

Emmie put her hands on her hips. "See what I mean."

"Alright, then." I let out a long breath. "That's me figured out. We find a way for me to get ahold of that inheritance somehow and I go off to I don't know where with the money. Then I find a doctor willing to hire me to do... anything really until I reapply for next year somewhere else." I closed my eyes for a moment. This was ridiculous. It didn't seem remotely possible. But what did I have to lose? I opened my eyes and faced Emmie. "What about you? What's your contingency plan?"

Emmie gave me a pained look. "I have no idea. If Hank proposes I suppose I could just..."

"Just be his wife? But you don't want to, do you?"

She shook her head. "I want to be something outside of that, but I don't know what."

"Didn't Hank say he'd heard of some big cities hiring female detectives? You do seem to be solving a lot of mysteries."

Emmie playfully elbowed me in the arm. "You mean *you* seem to be solving a lot of mysteries. You're the brains. I'm just the one who runs off and gets into trouble, looks for adventure."

"You have more brains than you give yourself credit for," I said. She only rolled her eyes. I continued, "But adventure. That's something we can work with. What would be adventure for you?"

Emmie shrugged. "I just know that I want it. That I want to be out there."

"Where is there?" I asked.

"I don't know."

"We can figure that out, too." I patted her on the shoulder. "We'll just devote some time to it while we're on our break."

Chapter 2

Emmie

We had reached the middle of all the celebration. Tents were pitched all over the field. Tiny old ladies displayed intricate quilts or tables laden with baked goods, and Farmer McPherson and his wife sold jars of apple preserves leftover from the fall. Fiddle players stood in an empty space, sawing away to claps and dancing.

Far in the distance was the viewing area for people of color, a reminder that the celebration wasn't a true celebration for all. White people like us got to attend for free, spending our money on the food and the airplane rides. We didn't have to pay to only be allowed to watch from a distance.

As we moved from tent to tent, I caught snatches of other people's conversations. Some of them mused on the lovely weather we had for Easter weekend. Others wondered, perhaps too loudly, if they might persuade McPherson to sell them some of "the good stuff." Prohibition hadn't stopped cider production one little bit. In fact, it had been explicitly allowed as a method of preserving apple harvests. And it was perfectly legal for McPherson and his wife to drink all the cider they wanted themselves, but selling it...you had to get a little more creative.

There was of course a fair amount of buzz about the planes and the flying—"Do you think we'll see any parachute jumping?"—but the main topic of conversation was the announcer and leader of festivities, Ellis Singleton.

Not that I got to see many movies, but apparently Ellis Singleton had starred in all the best ones. He'd played a knight in the crusades...who falls in love with a beautiful lady who faints in his arms. He'd played a daring spy...who falls in love with a beautiful lady who faints in his arms. He'd played a king who... well, same thing. And he'd been rumored to be stepping out with all these beautiful ladies and many more.

Dessa must have caught some of the conversation, too. "Do you think Agnes Lorraine will be here?" she asked.

Agnes was the beautiful lady that Ellis was seeing at the moment, and it was rumored that they were engaged to be married. "I hope so," I replied. "I'd rather see her than him." In Agnes' movies, she got to do more than faint and look glamorous.

"Me, too," said Dessa. "Did you know she does all her own stunts?"

"Really!" I was impressed. "Even in that scene when she dangled out of the airplane?"

Dessa nodded. "She did it. I hope she does come. Maybe she'll do an air stunt."

"Can she fly?" I asked.

"Not that I've read anywhere," said Dessa. "But you never know."

"You're right," I said. "Things are changing. Hank even had a female flight instructor in the war... not that she was actually allowed to fly into combat, but still some progress."

We wound our way through the crowd. We sampled some biscuits with apple preserves and headed away from the tents, toward a spot in the bright green grass where two figures stood beside a shiny biplane. I smiled. Hank adored planes. Everything about them. Maybe his friend would let him go up and I'd finally see him fly.

Dessa nudged me in the ribs. "That sounds like an adventure."

"What?"

She pointed ahead to the plane.

"You mean, me?"

"Why not?" she asked, her voice bright.

"I—um." Panic gripped my heart. I wiped my hands—which were suddenly sweaty—on my skirt. "Oh, I don't think so. That's Hank's thing."

"Really?" Dessa shot me a look of surprise. "It seemed like something that would interest you—like the motorcycle."

"No-no. I'm just—I'm definitely more of a motorcycle girl." Dessa stopped fixing me with her shrewd gaze and looked ahead. My shoulders loosened. Dessa thought I was all daredevil—and maybe I was a little—but the difference between the plane and my Harley was that my Harley was on the ground. The nice, safe, sturdy ground.

Ahead, Hank spotted us, waved, and came running up to meet us.

"You girls made it!" he cried, breathless. He ran one hand through his messy auburn hair. Hank grabbed each of us by the hand. "Come on. You have to meet Dewey Albright!"

Dewey? I looked to Dessa who was making the same puzzled expression I'm sure I was. I guess it was the association with the Dewey Decimal System, but the name Dewey conjured images of a quiet, unassuming person. Certainly not a war hero and a trick flyer.

We rushed to keep up with Hank's pace. Dessa tripped over a stick and almost fell. But in a few moments, we were panting, standing beside the red and white flying machine and before Dewey himself.

Dewey was tall, maybe an inch or two taller than Hank. He stood straight with his hands on his hips, enhancing his broad shoulders. In that pose, with goggles pushed up on top of his head, and dressed in a crisp, white shirt, he looked like a poster for an American pilot who had come home victorious.

"Good afternoon, ladies!" Dewey boomed in an appropriately deep and resonant voice. "Hank has told me so much about you."

"Hi!" I answered, a little breathless, and not only from the run. Hank had been a pilot of course—a darn good one, so I heard—but Dewey really looked the part. It was a little intimidating.

Dessa merely smiled and nodded.

Hank cleared his throat, his nose twitching. "This is Emmie," he said, taking my hand. "And this is Dessa."

"Lovely to meet you both," said Dewey with a grin. He motioned toward the massive machine behind him. "Care to have a look?"

We both hurried over to admire the wings, the paint job, to peer inside and see all the dials.

"This is a Curtis JN-4, Jenny for short," said Dewey.

I let out a whistle. Somehow all this metal could rise up off the earth and go soaring though the clouds. I still had trouble believing it. I turned to Hank, who was leaning casually against the side of the plane. "Is this what you flew in France?"

"We did fly Jennies, but this one here is a newer build," said Dewey. "Not a wartime hand-me-down. She's a civilian, meant for fun not fighting."

"I'm surprised more people aren't lining up to take a look," I said.

Dewey heaved a deep sigh. "I did have some earlier, but it seems that they are a little more interested in a certain celebrity." He paused to give a snort. "A celebrity who, I might add, hasn't even shown up yet."

Dessa, who had been eagerly examining the plane's interior, looked up in alarm. "He hasn't? I thought he was supposed to do opening announcements later this afternoon."

Dewey rolled his eyes. "He is. He should've been here hours ago. McPherson and everyone organizing this has been worried sick. They called the train station. They've called his agent all the way in Hollywood. No response. The train he should have taken arrived right on time this morning. No one at the station saw him get off. I don't think he ever got on in the first place."

I glanced away from the plane and back toward the crowds of busy people eating, drinking, and chattering together. "Well, they're going to be awfully disappointed."

Dewey huffed again. "I'm sure somebody else can announce. It's not like they aren't going to get a good show." He looked to me. "And I'm taking folks up in the plane tomorrow, if either of you girls would like a ride."

Dessa stood up a little straighter. "Oh, yes," she answered before I could even open my mouth. She motioned toward the plane. "Looks like we'll have to go one at a time, of course."

Dewey nodded. "Unfortunately, yes. There's only room for one passenger at a time."

I tried to slow my racing pulse. One at a time. Perhaps I could get Dessa to go first, and then when it was my turn, I'd find some excuse to get out of it altogether. Why did she have to be so interested in adventure all of a sudden?

I decided to change the subject. "Do you know the other pilots who'll be flying this weekend?"

"Well, I know Miles, of course. He'll be helping me with some stunts," said Dewey. "I've done some of these barnstormers before with Eugene, too. I don't know him well, but he's a good flyer. Apparently there is someone else coming. They should be here soon."

As if on cue, the roar of an engine drowned out the background noise of the crowd. I looked up. The tiny silhouette of the biplane against the bright blue sky grew larger and larger as the plane approached. The plane did a barrel roll, to applause from the crowd who now noticed its approach. Then the plane went in for a landing in the field some distance away.

"I guess that's the fellow," said Hank.

But even though we were quite far away, we were not so far away as not to notice when the pilot stepped out onto the grass and removed her helmet, letting down her mane of long, blonde hair. Her passenger emerged shortly afterward, and the two of them walked in our direction, carrying bags. Before I could clearly see their faces, I knew exactly who they were. Ellis Singleton and Agnes Lorraine arrived, as always, in style.

Chapter 3

Dessa

Ellis Singleton and Agnes Lorraine strolled through the long grass over to Dewey's plane, grinning from ear to ear. But when Ellis placed a hand on Agnes' shoulder, she shrugged it off.

Ellis surveyed the crowd some distance away, a crowd that was now moving closer. "I see the party has started without me," he said in a lazy drawl.

"Not everyone can wait for the likes of Ellis Singleton, apparently," said Agnes.

Ellis' smile flickered for a second, but he did not acknowledge the comment. Ignoring Dewey and Hank altogether, he focused his attention on Emmie and me. "Who are you two lovely ladies?" I felt my face grow red.

"I'm—" Emmie began, clearly feeling as awkward as I did, "we're just looking at the plane. Dewey's plane."

Agnes shot Ellis a look.

Dewey stepped forward and puffed out his chest. "That's right," he said. "They couldn't wait to see the real attraction at the air show."

I looked to Hank, wondering what he thought about all this. He watched the exchange, blinking and looking baffled.

Finally, the organizers of the barnstormer and the associated festivities reached this part of the field and rushed over to Ellis, peppering him with questions. Ellis shot us all a Hollywood smile and a wave and walked away, letting the organizers trail behind him as they talked.

Agnes leaned comfortably against the side of Dewey's plane. "Nice machine you've got here, D."

Dewey wrinkled his nose. I had a feeling no one else in the whole world called Dewey D.

"Better than your hunk of junk, Miss Lorraine," he answered in a strained voice.

Agnes ignored him and patted the plane affectionately "I look forward to seeing her in the air. Good day to you." Her gaze drifted to Hank, then Emmie, then landed on me, fixing me with her blue-eyed stare. "And all of you." She turned on her heel, tossing her long hair. After seeing her on the screen so many times, it was a little unreal to see her in person and to hear her voice instead of reading projected words. She wasn't one of the characters she played but the real living breathing Agnes. I glanced over my shoulder at Ellis retreating with the cluster of followers. Strangely, it hadn't felt as jarring to see him in real life. Instead, it felt like he was still on the screen. Still acting.

Someone else rushed over to the plane just then: a man with a briefcase, a ruffled suit, and a brown mustache that looked uncombed. His eyes bugged out and darted from left to right like a frightened squirrel. "Ellis! He was here! Where is he? Where'd he go? I'm his agent." The words tumbled from his mouth so fast I could barely catch them, and he aimed his speech at each of us, turning his head and pointing accusingly.

Hank recovered first. "He's—he's over there. Talking with some folks."

Without a word of thanks, the man ran off after Ellis, his briefcase flapping and hitting the side of his leg.

The general crowd was drawing closer now. Ellis and the air festival organizers had disappeared from view, perhaps into one of the barns to talk more privately. But attendees milled around the field, sniffing hopefully in the air. The agent darted away toward the outbuildings, in hot pursuit.

Hank checked his watch. "We should get something to eat" he said. "Things will be starting soon."

The biscuits and apple butter hadn't been a full meal, so we said our goodbyes to Dewey and headed back toward the tents where we could find something more substantial to eat.

As we strolled toward the smell of delicious roast chicken, Emmie said, "It's a long way to come for Ellis' agent."

"I suppose it is," I replied. "But I'm sure this isn't Ellis' only appearance out on the East Coast. I mean, barnstormer or no, he wouldn't have only booked one event in north Georgia."

Hank nodded. "They do these air shows in tours. Dewey said he has another one next weekend further north."

The crowd around me had a lot of strange faces. Our little town had plenty of open space, but certainly not enough people to make a barnstormer worthwhile. Instead, it was everyone from the surrounding bigger cities that made this appearance worth it. Folks came out from Athens or even as far away as Atlanta. I was certain every little inn and empty room in all of Cora, Georgia had been rented out.

"So, what is Dewey's issue with Agnes Lorraine?" asked Emmie. "It's one thing to not be a fan of her films, but he was downright rude."

"It's because…" Hank heaved a sigh. "I'm sorry ladies. It's because she's a woman who flies a plane. Do you remember the flight instructor I told you about?"

Emmie nodded. "Mrs. May, wasn't it?"

"That's right," said Hank. "Helen May. She's amazing. She knows more about airplanes than any man I've ever met. And if you'd been following aviation for a while, you'd certainly have known her name. I felt it was quite a treat to get to learn from her, but some of the fellows… Some fellows like Dewey didn't agree. He joked around in all her classes and he didn't pay attention. We all knew why. Dewey is a good pilot. But he could've been a better one if he listened to Helen May. I'm afraid he has the same attitude about any woman who flies."

Emmie's expression fell. And I felt just as deflated as I'm sure she did. This was the world that we lived in, and we were used to it, but the disappointment still stung.

Hank's next question deflated Emmie and me even further. "So, was there any mail for you today?"

* * *

We ate our dinners in a hurry and rushed toward the stage area, which was close to the biggest barn. We got lucky; we found spots near the stage, so we could see all the action.

The stage itself was draped in bright Easter colors. Flowers abounded. The crowd chattered eagerly as the festival organizers took the stage. I heard someone whisper, "When are we going to see Ellis?" and "Do you think he'll do autographs afterward?"

Finally, a man in a crooked bow tie stepped forward to the microphone they had rigged up. I was quite impressed by the system of wires and speakers. Though it was a large crowd, everyone would be able to hear everything. I wondered how far they had to run the wire to make it all work, though. Was this firesafe?

Through the crowd, I spotted Dewey standing close to the stage and chatting with someone else familiar. Ellis Singleton's agent leaned in and whispered something in Dewey's ear. They shook hands and parted, Dewey heading back towards the staircase at the back of the stage. Now, what was all that about?

The man with the crooked tie began. "We are pleased to present the first ever Cora, Georgia barnstormer!"

The crowd cheered and whooped. Cries of "Where's Ellis!" rang out. I could just picture Dewey's thunderous face, though he was out of my line of sight for now.

"We have excellent weather this Easter weekend 1920."

He waited. There were fewer cheers for Easter weekend 1920.

The announcer continued. "We have some dazzling pilots lined up, Dewey Albright, Eugene Mews, Miles Patterson." He took a pause. "And our final flyer, a lady pilot, Hollywood's Agnes Lorraine!"

Agnes Lorraine drew the loudest cheers of all. I could only imagine what Dewey thought about that.

"And finally," the announcer continued. "To narrate this astounding air show and the spectacular stunts we will see this weekend, actor extraordinaire Ellis Singleton."

The cheers were deafening as Ellis emerged onto the stage.

Ellis strode to the microphone and the festival organizers stepped aside. "Happy Easter weekend to all in Cora, Georgia!" Ellis began, then paused for the noise that followed. "I've traveled a long way to be here, but it was worth it to see this glorious countryside on today, Good Friday." More hollering of approval for the obvious pandering.

Ellis continued. "I am honored to welcome to stage our four fantastic pilots."

And that was it as they strode on stage. He didn't introduce them one by one. Not even Agnes. None of them looked happy, but Agnes had an expression full of thunder. Her bad mood broke, however, when she heard the chants of her name from the crowd. Someone shouted "Fly, Agnes!" She broke out into a big smile. Ellis on the other hand twitched his nose.

Ellis turned back to the crowd. "Who wants to see some of my most famous scenes performed live?"

They did. Oh boy, they did.

Ellis went on to reenact, as a one-man show, multiple death scenes from some of his more popular movies. I shifted from foot to foot and looked toward Hank and Emmie, who met my gaze with strained expressions. When were we going to get to the airplanes?

When, at one point, Ellis dramatically flopped to the ground to the stage with a bang, Dewey actually shouted, "Let's get a move on!" It drew a few laughs from the crowd and even some giggles from Agnes.

Ellis leapt to his feet, shot Dewey a look, and then brushed himself off. He cleared his throat. "And the moment we've all been waiting for this afternoon," he continued like nothing had upset him at all. "It's time for the first air stunt of the evening."

Agnes moved from her place on the stage, heading towards the staircase, but Ellis turned to her. "No, not you, darling." She returned to her spot, her face flushed and hands shaking.

"Our first stunt of the evening will be performed by Dewey Albright."

Dewey left the stage. Ellis grinned widely at the crowd. "While he's getting set up, how about some more scenes?"

A few more awkward one-man scenes later, Dewey's beautiful plane was circling overhead. Finally, the real show would begin. The crowd arched their backs, peering up the at the sky and cheering for Dewey's first swoop. A small sadistic part of me made me look back toward the stage to study Ellis' expression. He seemed crumpled. But Ellis continued to announce in a fluid, cheery voice as Dewey's plane made twists and turns, barrel rolls, and tricks I didn't know were even possible. At first it had looked to me like Dewey was flying around doing whatever came into his head, like a big, metal bird, but this was obviously planned in advance, because Ellis announced, "And now, folks, it looks like he's gearing up for the great swoop down. Yes, that's right, folks, this beautiful machine will be swooping down low right over your very heads."

I had been shifting my gaze between Ellis and the skies, but I stopped looking at Ellis at that point. I didn't want to miss the swoop. I heard Emmie give a little excited squeak beside me. I didn't doubt she was grasping Hank's hand. The plane approached, dipping lower, lower, and lower in the orange sky. Sunset would come soon. He'd better be finishing up before it got too dark.

"Here he comes" Ellis announced. "Can he do it?" The roar of the engine grew louder, drowning out the murmur of the crowd around me.

Swoosh. The plane passed low over our heads, low as top of a poplar tree. The crowd gasped as one. My chest tightened in a moment of fear for the tall roof of the nearby barn, but Dewey knew exactly what he was doing. He pulled up, soaring dramatically into the sky to whoops and cheers.

"He did it, folks!" Ellis shouted, sounding as enthused as any of us. "That was a close one, but he sure pulled it off." A rustling sound came from the speakers. Perhaps Ellis was pulling out whatever it was in his bag, but I wasn't looking. My eyes, like all of those in the crowd, were fixed on the red and white biplane now circling back.

Then a strangled cry came over the speakers. I whirled back toward the stage as Ellis Singleton dropped to the stage, covered in a wrinkly red flag. A red flag? Was what had been in the bag? I wracked my brain but couldn't think of a reason why. It must've been from one of his films I hadn't seen. Why would he pull out a red flag and drop to the ground?

But when Agnes raced forward, her face pale and terrified, I knew it was no scene. That's when I looked closer at the flag itself. Was that a little powder coming off it?

No. Oh no.

"Stop!" I shouted. No one could hear me. My chest tightened again. Agnes *needed* to hear this. I started again in a voice louder than I thought possible. "Stop!" I cried, pushing forward through the few people between me and the stage. I smelled it, now it made contact with Ellis' body. I was sure. "Don't go near. It's cyanide powder."

That got everyone's attention. The strangers in the crowd stepped aside as I moved even closer to the stage. Ellis lay unconscious on the stage floor. Agnes and the two remaining pilots walked towards me, giving Ellis a wide berth. Agnes crouched at the edge of the stage and pierced me with her blue-eyed gaze. The crowd was abuzz with noise, but I could hear her quite clearly as she quietly asked one question. "How did you know that?"

Chapter 4

Emmie

Several hours later, we sat in the parlor of the McPhersons' farmhouse, staring at apple after apple after apple. It seemed the McPhersons had a decorating theme. Not only did the house smell intensely of apple butter, but every picture on the walls depicted either an apple or an apple tree and every stick of furniture was upholstered in apple-printed fabric. Even some cushions on the sofa were sewn in the shape of apples. Everywhere one looked, there was another piece of shiny red or green fruit.

Outside, it had long since grown dark. The crowds were gone, and many of the folks the police had kept for questioning had been allowed to go as well. Now it was only me, Hank, and Dessa along with Agnes, Dewey, the other two pilots, Miles and Eugene, as well as Ellis Singleton's agent. Cecil Thorpe, his name turned out to be. Doctors had arrived quickly and taken extra precautions since, as Dessa had so rightly pointed out, the flag Ellis had pulled out at his bag had been covered in cyanide dust. He had been alive when the ambulance took away. But with that much cyanide absorbed through the skin and taken in his lungs, how could he possibly survive the night?

Miles and Eugene were being interviewed in one of the back rooms by Uncle Charlie and one of his deputies respectively, leaving the rest of us alone in the room together. Or rather in the room together while deputies stood just outside the door, making sure no one left. Agnes sat perched on the edge of her seat, still in her pilot's gear, an old shirtwaist and trousers, tapping the furniture with her hand. The entire evening she'd spent groaning about having to be here instead of sitting by Ellis' side. Yet she struck me as more annoyed than concerned for her beau who would almost certainly be dead by morning.

Agnes rose from her seat. "Why have we been shuffled into this room?" she asked to no one in particular. "I hate apples," she said under her breath.

Dewey looked around with a growing grin. "Well, I love apples. My favorite fruit. No, my favorite food of all time. I personally can't imagine a better room to be stuck waiting in." His eyes met Agnes' with a twinkle. Agnes sighed and returned to her seat.

Cecil shifted in his own seat. "I like apples as much as the next person," he said, "but the whole darn house is full of them. Can't the McPhersons find some other decorating inspiration?"

"You can say that again," Agnes agreed.

Dewey rose from his seat and strode about the room. "Come on, everyone, embrace the apple." He lifted a fruit from one of the many bowls placed around the room, walked over to Agnes, and waved under her nose. "Don't you want one? Surely you're getting hungry."

Agnes rolled her eyes. "No thank you." She gave him a little push and he backed away.

"Well, I'm starving," said Cecil. He reached for the nearest bowl, and simultaneously Hank, Dessa, and I all shouted *no*. But too late. He sunk his teeth into it...

And spit it back out all over the floor. Cecil gave a strangled cry. "It's fake!" He tossed the papier-mâché apple across the room.

There was a beat of silence before Hank shouted out what we were all thinking. "Of course, it's fake. It's April."

Cecil huffed and leaned back in his chair, crossing his arms over his chest. "We've got fresh ones in Los Angeles."

The rest of us in the room simply stared for a moment or two.

Agnes tossed her blonde curls. She focused her blue-eyed gaze on Hank and me but especially on Dessa. "Why are you three still here, Doctor Girl?"

"I—I'm not—" Dessa stammered. Agnes has been suspicious of Dessa's

22

explanation that she was studying to become a doctor. That's how she knew what the effects of cyanide poisoning looks like and how she could identify that it was most likely cyanide powder that had struck Ellis down. That and the smell. Not everyone can smell cyanide, but like Dessa, I could, and the bitter almond aroma was distinctive.

I couldn't have Agnes Lorraine bullying my friend, no matter how much of a celebrity she may be. "We're here because the sheriff asked us to stay," I said. "Just like you."

Cecil perked up at that moment and ran a hand through his disheveled hair. "But the sheriff is your uncle, right? I heard you call him that."

Agnes rounded on me now. "Oh, that's very convenient" she said. I chose to ignore it.

"Very convenient indeed," said Cecil, staring straight at me. "If someone wanted to get rid of a person."

Dewey stomped across the room and came to a halt in front of Cecil's chair. "What on earth would she have against Ellis Singleton? She's never met him before in her life." He gestured back to Dessa, Hank, and me. "Not any of them have."

Cecil stood and placed his hands on his hips. "I'm not saying any of them do have something against Ellis. But they could've been hired by someone who did."

Dewey laughed. "That's ridiculous!"

Cecil shrugged. "Is it?" He looked to Agnes.

Agnes rose from her chair again, breathing deeply and growing redder with every passing second, yet her voice was the same cool one she had used to question Dessa some hours ago. "What precisely are you implying?"

"I'm only saying—" But Cecil was interrupted, for as he took a step forward, he tripped over the same briefcase he'd been lugging around all day, which he had forgotten he placed at his feet. Cecil landed on the floor with an almighty thud just as the parlor door opened and a deputy let Eugene and Miles back into the room. The deputy cleared his throat. "You're all free to leave," he said. "But we will be in touch soon, so please don't leave town." Eugene and Miles hurried over to Dewey. Agnes rushed out of the room, muttering about getting to the doctor's house and who would give her a ride. Cecil scrambled from the floor and trailed after her, dusting himself off. His briefcase banged almost every person or piece of furniture he passed on the way out the door. As for Hank, Dessa, and myself, we made a beeline for Uncle Charlie.

We found him in the kitchen, having a big bite of biscuit with a dollop of apple butter. He smiled a little sheepishly when we came in, as he was mid-bite. He chewed, swallowed, and then said, "Hey, this is hungry work. I've had a long evening." He took his handkerchief from his pocket and wiped the biscuit crumbs from his pencil mustache. He put on a more serious expression. "Now, I know you three want to know everything, but—"

"I know you can't tell us everything," I finished for him. "But maybe a brief summary?" I flashed my most innocent smile.

"Now, Emmie, you know there's no such thing as a quick summary. You come barging in here, not thanking me for letting you all stay this late."

"But you did let us stay," I said, hopefully, "presumably so you could tell us something."

Uncle Charlie could resist the biscuit no more. He took another bite and spoke with his mouth full. "It was more that I wanted you to observe the others and tell *me* about them."

I moved closer and leaned on the edge of the kitchen table. "We can both tell each other things though, right? I *am* your favorite niece."

Uncle Charlie swallowed his biscuit and gave me *the look*. "You are my only niece."

"Exactly." I smiled. The corners of his mouth twitched. I had him.

"All right. Let's say I do agree to some exchange of information. It's going to be on my terms." He motioned to Hank and Dessa. "You two move out of the doorway. Shut the door and come closer before we chat." He gazed into each of our faces with his deep brown eyes. "What did y'all make of the main suspects."

A chill ran up my spine. The main suspects. It sounded so official, though I supposed it was. Only Ellis, the folks involved with planning the air show, and the people who had waited with us in the parlor would have had the opportunity to tamper with that bag. Uncle Charlie had let the local folks who worked on the air show go home pretty early. They obviously weren't high on the list. So, there it was. Agnes, the three male pilots, and Cecil, Ellis' agent. Five main suspects.

Hank spoke first, making me jump. I still startled whenever I saw the boy who was always so quiet in school speaking up with such a loud voice. Just one of the ways the war had changed him. "Dewey and Agnes know each other from before this," he said.

Uncle Charlie raised his eyebrows. "They told you that?"

Hank shook his head. "It was the way they acted. The way they talked to each other. I thought at first he disliked Agnes just because she was a female pilot. He's never mentioned her name to me. But seeing them together in the parlor tells me this is more than just his prejudice."

I looked to Hank in surprise. I hadn't picked up on that. But then Hank did know Dewey far better than I did.

"Agnes," said Uncle Charlie, "what do y'all think of her?"

"She didn't seem too worried about Ellis," I said. Hank and Dessa murmured an agreement.

"That she didn't," Uncle Charlie agreed. "But she did seem overly interested in you, Dessa."

"Me!" Dessa squeaked. "But—but—"

Uncle Charlie reached across the table and patted her hand. "It's all right. I'm not taking her seriously. But I do think she's looking for someone to blame. That's what it tells me. The question is whether she's looking for someone to blame because she's guilty or because she needs someone to direct her anger at."

I leaned forward. "That agent, Cecil, there's something odd about him."

Uncle Charlie nodded in agreement. "Anything else to add?" We told him about Cecil's implication that Agnes may have hired someone to try and kill Ellis. Uncle Charlie pulled a small notebook and pencil from his pocket and wrote it all down.

He cleared his throat. "Now I suppose I have to tell you all a little something before we go home. Well for starters they were all buzzing about backstage. None of them said they touched the bag. But unless this was an elaborate suicide, someone must be lying."

"How much cyanide was there?" I asked.

"I know what you're thinking," said Uncle Charlie. "You're wondering who would have been able to get that much? This being a farm, there were large stores of rat poison—cyanide—on the property. McPherson himself showed me where he kept it, and sure enough some was missing. Any one of them could've taken it."

"And Agnes and Dewey," said Hank, "didn't say that they knew each other when you questioned them?"

"No," Uncle Charlie replied. "Dewey, Miles, and Eugene all admitted to knowing one another from previous air shows, but all of them said they'd never met Agnes or Ellis before today. Agnes and Ellis know each other, obviously. And Agnes and Cecil know each other, but both of them said they'd never met any of the other pilots."

Speaking of Cecil, that was bothering me. "What is Cecil doing out here, anyway? It's a long way for him to travel."

Uncle Charlie nodded. "That seemed off to me too. Cecil says he's here because Ellis requested it."

"Why did Ellis request that?" asked Dessa.

"According to Cecil," said Uncle Charlie, "Ellis refused to say. Cecil, valuing his job, simply obeyed."

"And he wasn't supposed to fly here, was he?" I asked. "Everyone was really surprised when he showed up in Agnes' airplane instead of taking the train."

"That's somewhat debatable," said Uncle Charlie. "All the locals in charge expected him at the station. Cecil expected him at the station. Agnes, however, said that it had always been the plan for him to fly with her. So, who's lying? Or who's confused? Why?" It was a puzzle. I supposed that Ellis had made a last-minute change to make a dramatic entrance. But why should Agnes lie about it if that were the case?

"I've kept everyone here long enough," said Uncle Charlie. "It's time that the three of you, at least, go home and get some rest." He took his jacket from where it lay on the table "Emmie, I assume you took your bike?"

I nodded. "I did. Me and Dessa. But, Hank, you got a ride with someone, right?"

"That's right," said Hank.

"All right, then. Emmie, you take Hank home in the sidecar. I'll drive Dessa back and try to smooth things out with her parents."

"Thank you," Dessa breathed. I could almost see her muscles relax. It hadn't occurred to me, but she must have worried the whole evening about what they would say with her returning so late. If, of course, they were currently in a mood to notice where she'd been at all.

We were just about to head for the door, when Uncle Charlie reached out a hand. "One last thing. I know you three have been involved in investigations before, and I know you've got an interest, maybe even an aptitude. I also know you're not going to listen when I tell you to stay out of the way for your own safety. Maybe you'll listen to this. The way things are going I don't think I'll be sheriff much longer."

What! I couldn't have heard that right, could I? "Why?" I cried, a little too loudly. Uncle Charlie shushed me.

"It doesn't go beyond this room, but well it doesn't need to. Things are changing in Cora, not necessarily in the direction I want them to. And folks have always considered me a bit progressive for the area." He chuckled. "And I've not done that half the things I wanted to do. But the point is I'm going to have a difficult election coming up. I'm happy to talk with you, to share information privately, and I'm happy to have you tell me when you find something amiss. But be careful. Mostly for yourselves, but also because it doesn't look good to have you three seeming to run the investigation. I can just tell what people would say."

I could just imagine as well. We nodded and agreed. If we did any sleuthing, we'd keep it very quiet. This time Uncle Charlie led the way toward the door, but we weren't two steps into the hallway when one of the deputies popped in, his face pale and alarmed.

Uncle Charlie wrinkled his forehand. "What's wrong?"

The deputy shook his head sadly. "The doctor just called. Ellis Singleton is dead. This is now a murder case."

27

Chapter 5

Dessa

The sun seemed to rise far too early on Saturday morning. I dressed in a hurry and slipped downstairs, hoping my parents would be too busy with Easter plans for their various committees and functions to have lingered long over breakfast. I headed for the kitchen, hoping to duck in, grab some bread and butter, and sneak back upstairs. I hadn't taken two steps in that direction when my mother's voice called out.

"Odessa!" I flinched. I hated it when she used my full name.

I knew better than to refuse to answer. "Yes, Mother?"

"Come in here, darling." There was an edge to her voice as she said the word *darling*. Charlie had done his best the night before to smooth things over when he dropped me off at the ungodly hour of one in the morning, but there was still more to be said.

My heart leapt to my throat. I turned and walked slowly toward the dining room, my footsteps echoing on the hardwood floor. Both my parents sat at either end of the long dining table. The breakfast dishes, plate of biscuits, bowl of dried fruits, sliced ham, soft-boiled eggs, jam, and coffee in a pot sat between them against the backdrop of the lace tablecloth. I took a seat along one side, edging my chair close to the middle of the table, not wanting to be particularly close to either one of them at the moment.

Flossie must've heard me come downstairs. She entered now, bringing me a plate, and she served up my usual breakfast of buttered biscuit and a black coffee. I didn't like much early in the day.

"Thank you," I muttered when she set the plate before me.

My father began without preamble. "I don't want you leaving the house today, running about all over McPherson's farm with Miss McAllister."

I expected as much, but I still felt the need to object. "It's not like she killed him."

My mother sat down her empty coffee cup with a flourish. "That's hardly the point. I don't want you wrapped up in another murder investigation. Your progressive friends are quite scandalous enough. We don't need anything more for people to talk about. Not when I've got two young men for you to meet after school is back in session."

I steadied myself before replying. "How soon?" I asked in a small voice.

My mother peered over her reading glasses at me. "I hope it will be the first and second weekend after you return to school. I know that attaining this two-year degree has become the fashionable thing, but if you were home…"

I opened my mouth to reply, but my father got there first. "There's no use arguing that anymore. She's almost finished it anyway."

It had been a long two years, first convincing my parents to allow me to pursue the degree to begin with, pitching it as an enticement for a potential husband and a way to increase ties with the Lucy Cobb Institute. But every time my schooling became inconvenient for them, one or the other would balk at it. But now, only three months from graduation, my father was right. There was no point arguing. If I left now, it would make them look worse, not better. Plus, the tuition had already been paid.

I chose my next words carefully. "Speaking of potential romantic interest, I was wondering something."

My parents each lifted their eyebrows in surprise. "You were?" asked my mother. "You've never taken interest in matters of the heart before. I'm pleased to see a change."

Oh yes, I have. I thought. *But their names were Teresa and Birdie.* I bit my lip to suppress a hysterical giggle. Wouldn't that explode everything.

My father took a long drag of a cigarette and blew out the smoke. "I'm glad of it too. You've spent far too much time in your room studying anatomy texts." He spat out the word *anatomy* like it was something disgusting. Indeed, he had personally ripped out certain pages of my textbook, deeming them unfit for proper female eyes. Not that I was interested in those particular pages anyway.

"What were you wondering?" asked Mother.

I took a deep breath. This part of this conversation had to go just so. I could've kicked myself. Why did I choose this moment to broach the subject? The night before had already upset them so much. But I began, so I had to finish. Honestly, they seemed so happy, sitting up straighter, eyes brighter, now that I had taken even the slightest interest in marriage. As much as I hated the box they wanted to shut me in, they were still my parents. And deep inside, a part of me felt guilty that I would never, could never, live up to their expectations. I began. "I know that Granddad left a sum of money for me in anticipation of my wedding." I stopped there, unsure how to go forward. I scrunched the napkin in my lap and let the silence stretch for a moment, hoping they would meet me where I wanted to go.

My father frowned. "Indeed, he did. And we have kept it safe for you all this time. What is your question?"

Now I had to ask it. Not everything I needed to know, but something. "I was wondering how much." My voice grew faster of its own accord as I fiddled with the napkin in my lap. "Not that it's appropriate to discuss such matters over the breakfast table, but I thought it might be helpful to get a sense, to know where things stood." Didn't make sense? I hoped so.

"Indeed, this is a delicate subject for the dining room," my father said. "But," he conceded, "you're twenty years of age, and it is only fitting that you understand something of your financial situation. Your grandfather left you two thousand dollars. I recommend an appropriate but not overly indulgent ceremony and celebration, with most of the money used to give you and your husband a decent financial start in life."

I nodded. My hands began to unclench under the table as the napkin fell limply to my lap. "Thank you for telling me, Father." That was it. But it was a start. Two thousand dollars. *Thousand.* Surely that much money was in a bank account in my father's name, not secreted somewhere in a place that I could access independently. My heart sank, and I took another sip of coffee to cover my expression. What had I expected? That he would move a painting and open a hidden safe?

My mother and father pushed back their plates and stood up from the table. "Your father and I both have plenty to do in anticipation of the Easter events tomorrow," said Mother. "I'd like to repeat that we need you to stay here today without any potential investigations. Your aunt is coming this afternoon. Take this time to prepare for her arrival."

That was right. Aunt Margaret was coming this afternoon. With the chaos of Ellis Singleton's death and my own backup plans on my mind, I had completely forgotten about her. Just what I needed, more to do. And I hadn't seen Aunt Margaret in over ten years. To me, she was an unknown entity. Would this additional person make things even more tense?

Just then I heard a knock on the front door and Flossie's quick footsteps as she hurried to answer it. Then came Charlie's voice, "I need to speak with Mr. and Mrs. Child, please."

I pushed back my chair and stood, heart thumping. After everything that happened yesterday evening, what could possibly be wrong now?

Uncle Charlie was in the dining room in a flash. He nodded and turned to each of my parents. "Mr. Child, Mrs. Child, I'm sorry to disturb your breakfast, but as Dessa was a key witness of what happened yesterday, and as a she has some rudimentary medical knowledge, I'm afraid I need to speak with her for a time as a part of our investigations." My parents looked at one another and then back at Charlie.

"And what exactly do you need to ask my daughter?" asked my father with a smile, but also with a hard edge to his voice.

Charlie smiled in return shook his head. "I'm afraid I'm not at liberty to say. But if she'd like to come down to the station, I am certain she would be of great assistance."

My parents exchanged a glance, weighing their options. If what Charlie told us the night before was true, that he was likely to be voted out in the next election, they might see it as a point of weakness, and feel free to deny his request. On the other hand, the election had not occurred. Charlie was still the sheriff.

"Then, I suppose she must accompany you," my father said with a sigh. He crossed his arms. "My sister arrives on the train at four o'clock this afternoon. I hope very much that Dessa can be home in time for her arrival."

"Of course." Charlie smiled. "I am certain we will be wrapped up in plenty of time."

I nodded to each of my parents and followed Charlie out of the house and through the green spring grass to the police car that waited. I climbed into the passenger seat as he got into the driver's side.

"I didn't think I'd overlooked anything yesterday," I said quickly. "Did some new information come to light?"

Charlie turned and gave me a slow smile. "Not at all. But that got you out of the house, didn't it?"

For a moment I was speechless, my mouth hanging inelegantly open. Then Charlie began to chuckle, and soon I couldn't help but join him. He started the car and pulled out into the road.

"So," Charlie began as he drove through the streets of our little town, still abuzz with visitors, despite everything that happened the day before, "I'm guessing you haven't had a letter from the university either?"

"No," I said, "and I –" and then it all spilled out. Emmie's and my plan. Not for her. Her own contingency plans were her story to tell if she wanted. But I explained our plan for me. The money that was mine but wasn't. The fact that I wasn't staying in my parents' house a moment longer than I had to. The way that the situation still seemed rather hopeless. Charlie nodded and listened as he drove.

"That's a tricky one," he said. "But I'm not the person to ask about this. If there's ever anyone to help you figure out how to get a hold of that money, it's the ladies who I have a feeling are in my kitchen chattering right now." We pulled up beside Emmie's house and climbed out of the car. I felt lighter with relief. He was right. A few pots of coffee or tea and between all of us, we'd have this figured out. And at any rate, it was something to do that had nothing to do with solving a murder. I followed him hurriedly up the path to the front door.

Chapter 6

Emmie

I hurried to the parlor window when I heard the rumble of the police car's engine close by. By the time I pushed the lace curtains aside and looked out, Uncle Charlie and Dessa were already crossing the lawn. I called over my shoulder, "The trick worked!"

"Good!" came Granny's voice. "The way those spiteful parents keep that girl—a grown woman—locked up is ridiculous." Granny waddled into the parlor, coffee cup in hand.

Hank and his mother Miss Ethel weren't far behind. The ringing telephone filled the house with noise. I heard the clatter of footsteps, Momma rushing to answer it.

Uncle Charlie and Dessa came into the house and joined us.

"I got her free and delivered her to safety," said Uncle Charlie. "But I'm afraid I can't stay to chat. Still on a murder case." He waved and made for the front door when Momma's voice called out.

"Charlie! Wait! It's the station, on the telephone for you."

Uncle Charlie frowned and turned on his heel. He hurried to the back of the house where the telephone was.

"Maybe there really is a new development," said Dessa.

Momma joined us in the parlor, swirling her own coffee cup absentmindedly. A few drops escaped and fell to the floor. She looked down at the tiny, round brown spots and frowned.

"Did they tell you anything?" asked Miss Ethel.

Momma shook her head. "Whatever it is, it seemed urgent."

We didn't have long to wait in suspense. Uncle Charlie rushed back through, making a beeline for the front door. He didn't even look our way, but simply called out, "Dewey's done a runner. He could be anywhere now."

"So, he's the guilty one?" asked Momma.

Uncle Charlie paused just for a moment as he wrenched open the front door. "Not necessarily." He shook a finger in her direction. "We can't make assumptions, but when people disappear during a murder investigation that usually means one of two things." He stepped out into the spring sunshine and shut the door behind him so swiftly it was almost slammed. Through the window, I saw him practically jog to the car.

He did not need to say what those two things were. Most likely, Dewey was either guilty or dead.

I turned to Hank. His face had grown red. "He didn't do it," he said in a low voice, shaking his head.

I placed one hand delicately on his arm. "Are you sure—?"

He cut me off. "He did not do it."

I nodded. Hank was convinced. And I guessed that when you served with someone in a war, you got to know them pretty well. Still, there was no telling who Dewey had become since the war. But I knew better than to point that out to Hank. And then there was the other possibility. If Dewey was not guilty, was he still among the living? The temperature in the room seem to have dropped dramatically. I sank into a wingback chair.

Granny sat down her cup on a side table with a thud and clapped her hands loudly. "I know what we all need. Back to the barnstormer!"

Dessa stared, eyes wide. "Surely it's not still happening!"

Granny put her hands on her hips. "Oh, it's happening. You don't get a town to work for months in advance, get all those folks coming in from South Carolina, from Atlanta. You don't do all that and then cancel over one dead body. Besides," she lifted one corner of her mouth. "With the murder, it's bound to get a lot more interesting."

That was Granny for you. If she didn't spend so much of her retired years traveling from place to place, visiting one group of friends and the next, she would have solved the last two murder mysteries Dessa and I had been involved with. Solved it in a day. But she had missed all the excitement while she was off chasing excitement somewhere else, having been out of town for the first murder in the woman's club and having gone to visit a friend in the mountains instead of coming with us to Savannah last summer. I got the impression that she was a bit disappointed that when she was around everyone seemed to be perfect law-abiding citizens. So, it was no surprise that she quickly gathered her bag and bundled us all up in sweaters. "It will be chilly later" she said, then practically pushed us out the door and in the direction of the McPhersons' farm.

"You don't want us to take the motorcycle and sidecar?" I asked, wistfully looking over my shoulder at the shiny green machine as Granny marched us down the sidewalk.

"Nonsense," Granny barked. "A brisk walk will do us good." A brisk walk indeed. It would take us nearly an hour to get there on foot. But as we were already a block away there was no arguing now.

I breathed in the fresh, flower-scented air and tried to enjoy the scenery. The late-season daffodils nodded their flowery heads in the wind. Birds chirped in the trees overhead. Spring was truly here. I imagined the festivities of the following day, the church service, the egg hunt, the delicious food to be had at home afterward. And, of course everyone in their Easter finery, including—for the ladies—their largest, most floral hats. My mother had an impressively large head adornment saved just for tomorrow. I looked at her head now and contrasted the soft, shady blue hat she wore with tomorrow's bonnet in my mind. I couldn't help but smirk.

Momma knit her eyebrows. "Why are you looking at me so strangely?" Her sharp voice pierced the morning quiet. "Yesterday you were like elephants on the staircase. Today you stare at me like some sort of monkey. I wonder what animal you will be on the way home. I didn't raise you to act like a zoo, Emmeline McAllister."

Granny snorted. "Oops," she said, blushing. "I guess I'm the pig."

Momma rolled her eyes at her own mother. "And you just encourage her," she grumbled.

We passed through the main streets of the town, which were as busy they had been the day before. Granny was right. The murder wasn't putting anyone off. And in a way that was a relief. There were a lot of businesses counting on the folks from out of town to stay and spend their money

In the pre-Easter crowd, I spotted someone familiar. I tapped Hank and Dessa each on the shoulder. I pointed. "Is that Cecil skulking over there by the general store?"

They both squinted in that direction. Hank raised a hand and shaded his eyes. "Yes, I think so," he said.

The man I was certain was Cecil stepped onto the sidewalk, looked both ways, and crossed the road, a bulky briefcase banging against his leg as he went. Yes, definitely Cecil.

"I'm dying to know what's in that briefcase," said Dessa. Hank and I looked at her with questioning eyes.

Dessa shrugged. "I understand why he had it yesterday, if he had come just from the train station. Or if he was using it as a primary piece of luggage. And he could have had it yesterday because he had some documents or something that Ellis needed to see. But what does he need it for now?"

"Maybe Ellis left everything to Agnes," said Hank. It was a good point. We had no clue who inherited all of Ellis' money. If it was Agnes, it would explain the presence of the briefcase and give her a motive for the murder.

Dessa shook her head. "Surely Cecil would have handled that first thing in the morning. But even if he waited, with all that Hollywood money, I'm certain he could have rented a car. But here he is on foot running around downtown, dragging his briefcase everywhere."

She was right. Sure enough, Cecil wasn't headed to any car parked along the streets. Maybe he just liked the walk, but somehow I didn't think so.

"Let's stop at the general store on the way," I whispered, "ask Silas what he was up to in there."

Momma spun around so fast I was surprised she didn't fall over with dizziness. She shook her finger in my direction. "That's snooping!" she said as she walked backwards, not missing a beat.

I shrugged. "Maybe it is, but it's not any more snooping than anyone else in this town does."

Granny let out another piglike snort. "The girl has got a point."

Momma folded her arms across her chest, still walking backwards. I was impressed. If it were me trying that, I'd have fallen over three times by now, but Momma navigated the cracks and uneven paving in the sidewalk like she walked backwards over it every day. "Fair enough," Momma conceded, "but remember what your uncle said. Be careful what you say. No making it seem like anything more than ordinary nosiness." She turned around at last and picked up the pace, mumbling about busybodies as she went.

We entered the general store en masse. Old Silas nodded to us from behind the counter.

"What can I do for you?" he muttered through his bushy, gray mustache.

I stepped up the counter. "A pack of gum, please." I said, ignoring Momma's *tut-tut* behind me. She detested gum chewing, but it was the only item that came to mind.

"Anything else?" Silas mumbled.

"One for me as well, please," said Granny.

Wordlessly, Silas turned to the shelves behind him. The dingy shelves were packed with items of all kinds, with no particular organization that I could discern. But it clearly made sense to Silas. He went right to the gum—he only carried one brand—, removed two packs, and placed them on the counter. Anyone else might have though Silas' unchanging expression or terse conversation meant that he was angry. But that was just his way with everyone all the time. Silas liked me. Or I thought he did. He was the one who sold me my motorcycle, at quite a steal of a price, too. Of course, I'd had to finish putting the thing together myself.

"So, I was wondering, Silas…" I said. Granny took that moment to nudge me gently in the arm. She looked at me with an expression that said *May I?* I nodded. *Go right ahead, Granny. It's your turn.*

"We were wondering," said Granny, "with all these visitors in town, if that agent had popped in here recently. The one from Hollywood." A smile spread over her face. Her eyes sparkled. My granny was having the time of her life.

Silas stroked his mustache. "Sure did. Just now."

Granny set down the money to pay for the gum. "He was just shopping or...?"

Silas gave her change without a word.

Miss Ethel stepped up and gave it a try. "There was nothing to worry about with that agent coming in here, right?"

Silas shut the cash register drawer with a clang and the jingle of coins. "Nothing to concern yourself with." His voice, as always, carried no emotion. He might be angry with us; he might be afraid and protecting himself or even us. I couldn't tell. Silas turned his back to us and began straightening items on the disorganized shelves. The interview was over. We stepped back outside.

"So, what do you think?" asked Miss Ethel as we trotted down the sidewalk once again in the spring sunshine. "Is Cecil running booze?"

"Could be," said my mother.

I tried not to look, but my eyes kept being drawn in Dessa's direction. She blushed and looked at the ground. If anyone would know about that, her mother would. Not that I ever wanted to ask Dessa to question her mother about that issue.

Granny had a different opinion. "You silly girl!" She shook her finger playfully at Miss Ethel. I did my best not to snicker at the sight of anyone, even my grandmother, calling Hank's mother a silly girl. "Cecil came out here all the way from California. That's an awfully long way to go to run booze. There are local sources for that."

Miss Ethel looked a bit sheepish and we were all quiet for a moment as we walked on. Cecil was up to something. But it probably wasn't booze.

And thinking of luggage that got dragged everywhere, I couldn't help but watch Granny's enormous bag swing back and forth banging her against the leg the same way Cecil's briefcase banged him. "What on earth is in that bag, Granny?"

Granny chuckled. "It's a doozy." She stopped still on the sidewalk and turned around. She pulled the bag from her shoulder up close to her. "Do y'all want to see?"

When we all replied that of course we did, she ignored Momma's protests of "This is a public sidewalk" and "We're blocking the flow of foot traffic" and opened her leather bag. She pulled out something extraordinary: a gorgeous, shiny, leather and metal device. A camera. A real camera of her very own. I whistled. I couldn't help it. It was beautiful.

"That is gorgeous," Hank muttered. And Dessa wordlessly put a hand on its shiny surface and gasped.

"Do you know how to use it?" I asked.

"Do I know how to use it!" Granny laughed, and I'm sure I would've got a finger wag if she had not been holding the precious camera. "Of course, I know how to use it. I've developed some photographs already. And I'm bringing it with me today to document our first air show." She nodded toward Miss Ethel. Miss Ethel had run our tiny town's newspaper—some might call it a leaflet—making note of the events in Nowheresville, Georgia once a week for I don't know how many years. Photographs were few and far between. This was a big step up for the Cora Gazette.

Granny packed the camera away again, closing her bag with an affectionate pat, and we hurried again on our way.

"I can't believe I didn't know about this," I said. "Did you get it on your last trip out of town?"

"Sure did," Granny said. "You will have to help me when we get to the air show. I might even let you take a picture or two."

After a long hike, we finally arrived back at the air show. The farm was as busy as it had been the day before. After wading through the crowd and listening in to their conversation, full of ghoulish theories about Ellis' murder, Granny took out her camera again and began preparing to snap photos.

Momma and Miss Ethel trotted off with their notebooks and pencils, ready to chat with folks for the newspaper. Granny motioned for Hank, Dessa, and I to gather around her. "Come see how this works, young'uns."

Granny took a few shots of the crowd. Then, to my surprise, she handed the precious camera right to me. "Give her a whirl," she said.

The camera was surprisingly heavy in my hands. "Are you sure?" What if I broke it?

Granny patted me on the shoulder. "You saw how I did it. I trust you. Take a shot." And so I did take a few pictures. I still had no idea what the other side of this process looked like. Didn't you have to develop the photos with some liquid? In a dark place? Where was Granny going to do that in our house? Nevertheless, taking the pictures was... fun. To think that you could open a tiny little window for just a fraction of a second, let in the light, and that would make a picture that looks exactly like what you're seeing. I thought back to the art classes Dessa and I had taken at Lucy Cobb. Dessa, of course, had followed instructions to a T. And she had excelled, producing beautiful still lifes and lovely botanical illustrations. I, on the other hand, was a little more frustrated. Our teacher had encouraged my creativity, but there was something more I wanted. A realism my fingers couldn't capture, and a sense of immediacy. The quick clicks of the camera felt right. Granny's hand rested on my shoulder.

"All right, then. Slow down," said Granny. "We've got to save some film for the airplanes." I lowered the camera and handed it back to Granny, feeling my face go warm.

"Sorry. Of course."

We climbed the steep green hill toward the planes. A spring breeze whooshed down upon us from the bright blue sky. All this color. It was a shame that the camera wouldn't capture that as well.

Lines had already formed for Eugene and Miles to take people up on airplane rides. Hank nudged me in the ribs. "Wouldn't that be a fun place to take pictures?" He asked. I peered up at one of the airplanes buzzing overhead, a tiny silhouette against the sky.

"In – in," my voice was shaking. "In the plane?"

"In the sky," Hank breathed, staring up with longing.

"Imagine the wonderful pictures," came Dessa's voice from my other shoulder. "It would be like giving a bird a camera."

Granny hugged her camera bag to her side. "I am certain it would," she said, "but we won't find that out today. Not a one of you is taking my camera into an airplane."

Phew. I took a few deep breaths, and my heart began to slow down. That was one less reason for people to push me into an airplane. Maybe, with everything going on this weekend, I would get through the whole thing without having to so much as sit in one.

"Look over there!" Hank pointed across the field. There she was, in a comically large coat despite the warm spring weather, probably hoping that no one would notice her. Agnes Lorraine strode away from her airplane followed by Cecil and his ever-present briefcase. She turned to him, seeming to be talking, then waved her hand as in a dismissal. She turned away again and hurried onward. Cecil scuttled in the other direction.

"We should go talk to her," said Hank, then he added sheepishly, "You know, for the paper."

"Oh yes, indeed." Granny straightened up.

"I don't know." Dessa frowned. "She's probably just trying to get a bite of lunch without anyone bothering her. Look how she's hiding under that coat."

"Yes, dear, she probably is," said Granny in a softer voice, "but this is the best chance we'll get. We may not have another."

"All right then," I said. Obviously either I or Granny or both of us would go. It was just a matter of what to ask.

But before I could take a step forward Hank said, "It should be Dessa."

"What?" I said, and Granny echoed my surprise. Dessa had done some brave things in the past, but she was not a natural conversationalist. She should be telling us what to ask, not doing the asking.

Dessa, for her part, was shrinking into herself. She hunched her shoulders so much I thought she might risk injury as she attempted to look smaller and smaller. "No," she squeaked. "Agnes hates me."

Hank turned and placed a hand on Dessa's shoulder. "Yes, I know. And that's exactly why it has to be you. She'll be angry when she sees you. If she's angry, she might let something slip that she hasn't told the police."

"But—but—" Dessa had grown pale. But I could see something else in her face, a spark of interest. Hank had a good point. But could Dessa pull it off? Or would we be picking her up off the field where she fainted in her attempt?

41

Chapter 7

Dessa

He couldn't be serious. I couldn't do it. I could barely speak to my parents that morning. I'd be happy to tell them what questions to ask. Or just be there if my presence was what was needed. "I could just go along?"

Please. Please, don't make me do this. If a life full of secrets had taught me anything, it was to keep your head down. Do what you're supposed to do. Don't let anyone notice you.

Hank patted my shoulder. "I know it's hard for you. But you can do this. If I can do this, so can you."

He gave me a rare smile. But I couldn't quite meet his gaze. I hoped I could do it.

But maybe he had a point. Hank had always been distant with me. For a long time, I thought he didn't like me, either because I spent so much time with Emmie or because he didn't approve of my liking girls. But the more time I spent with him, the more I realized that he and I were very much alike. I had known Hank my whole life but until I became Emmie's friend, we hadn't spoken much. Before the war, Hank didn't speak to much of anyone except for Emmie. He had come home different. He'd had to learn to speak up and do things that were difficult. And I probably wouldn't have approached Agnes if anyone else had asked me to do it. At least Hank knew exactly what he was asking of me.

I nodded shakily. "All right. Here I go." I hurried through the tall grass in her direction, not daring to look back, not to daring to think too hard about what was coming, not daring to even think about the questions ahead of time. I put one foot in front of the other. One step at a time, walking as though in a dream.

I put on some speed to catch up with Agnes, calling out to her and taking out the small notebook and pencil I always carried in my bag or pockets. She only turned up the collar of her large coat and hurried forward. I forced my voice to be louder, then louder still, finally adding, "It's Dessa Child, from yesterday." Still no response. "I knew it was cyanide."

She stopped so fast I almost ran into her. Agnes spun around, then jumped back, startled that I was so close. I stepped back a little too.

Agnes looked me over from my flyaway hair to the notebook I carried. "What's that for?" She pointed.

"The newspaper," I replied automatically. I forced myself to keep my voice audible. "I'm helping them out."

Agnes snorted. "Doctor girl, police girl, now newspaper girl too? What don't you do in this town?"

"It's a small town." I didn't have to force my voice so much this time. I was beginning to feel something other than nervousness. What was it? Was it annoyance? There was something about her tone. The sneer on Agnes' lovely face. Yesterday I had been too carried away by her star status to really notice it, but Agnes walked into every room and crowd like she was the best person there, like it was a duty for her to put up with anyone else. I couldn't imagine she and Ellis having a very happy courtship. After all, can two people be the best?

"I already told the police all I'm going to say," said Agnes. "You can get your information from them." She turned on her heel

"Wait!" I cried, my voice again dying over the drone of the wind. I tried again. "Wait!" I was losing the opportunity. A thought struck. "I just wanted to see how you were doing."

That one worked. She turned and faced me again, practically shaking with fury.

"My fiancé's dead, murdered in front of me. I'm being hounded by his lousy excuse for an agent. The police keep bothering me. Now, you, the little poison expert, turn up. How do you think I'm doing?"

I had a split second. *Remember, push her. Don't ask questions the police could find out easily.*

"So..." My voice died away again. No. No. Hank thought I could do this. I was going to do this. I had to think quick. What didn't make sense. And I had it. I said it aloud before I even thought about how loud my voice was. "Why keep the flag in the bag?"

"What?" Agnes blinked at me. It clearly wasn't the question she expected either.

"The flag Ellis used. It's so much easier to carry it without a bag, and especially awkward on stage. Why did he ever put it in there in the first place?"

All the tension and anger seem to fall away from Agnes then as she pondered the question herself. "No idea. It doesn't make any sense. But he seemed determined to keep it there. He kept an eye on that bag at all times, hardly ever setting it down since we left California." She came back to herself and seemed to remember that she was angry at me. She narrowed her eyes. "So that's where the killer is, most likely. In the California. Not here. Not me. You can all stop wasting everyone's time." She stalked off again and this time I let her go. Maybe the killer really was back there, across the country. What if, instead of none of the suspects having an alibi, almost all of them did? But it was only Agnes' word we had for any of it.

* * *

Emmie

I watched Dessa walk away unsteadily. "Are you sure that was a good idea?" I asked Hank.

He smiled. "She'll be fine. Worst case, Agnes yells at her, but she can handle it."

I squinted at Dessa in the distance, heard her call Agnes' name. Agnes turned around.

"I guess she can take it from here," I muttered.

Granny shuffled her feet. "She sure can," she said in a reassuring voice. "Your little friend is tougher than she knows. But in the meantime, what about us? What do we do besides stand awkwardly in this field?"

Fair point. We really shouldn't gawk at them for the whole interview. I cast my eye about the field. Miles' plane was in the air, but Eugene had landed, his passenger stepping off.

I pointed. "We should go talk to him. Maybe he can make some time for us in between flights."

We rushed over. There was quite a crowd waiting to take a ride, and some of them gave us dirty looks for appearing to cut the line, but Granny took out her camera and yelled "Press!" and the crowd parted.

"Press?" muttered Eugene absently, making checks on the plane. Then he looked up and saw who was coming. "Oh good. It's you!" he said to Hank. He offered apologies to the next person in line and assured her it would only be a few minutes.

He motioned for us to follow him around to the other side of the plane, where the waiting crowd couldn't hear. "It's Hank, right?"

Hank nodded.

"I'd been hoping to see you today," said Eugene. He frowned at Granny's camera. "I didn't know you were with a newspaper, though."

"It's only me who's with the paper, really," said Granny. "And it's more of a neighborhood weekly letter than anything. Don't worry, young fellow." She patted Eugene on the arm. "We know when it's best to be discreet."

Eugene's shoulders relaxed. "That's alright then. If we can keep it out of the paper, I'd like to talk about Dewey."

"Of course." Granny nodded. Then she added, with a wink, "As long as we can get a good shot with you and this gorgeous flying machine when you're done."

Eugene smiled. "Naturally."

Hank frowned and stuck his hands in his pockets. "About Dewey. I know you were friends."

Eugene nodded. "We've done quite a few of these barnstormers together in the last few years. You knew him during the war, right?"

"That's right," said Hank. "He didn't say anything to you before he took off?"

Eugene shook his head. "That's what I was going to ask you. He never told me a thing. And that's what makes me so worried, because I know Dewey. He's no killer."

We stood silent a moment, letting the ambient sounds of the airplane overhead and the din of the crowd fill the space that words couldn't. Hank seemed to sag. He knew as well as I did what that probably meant.

I broke the silence at last. "I believe you, but it might help to know why he seemed to hate Ellis so much. Did they know each other from someplace?"

Eugene shrugged. "I don't think so. He was never fond of actors being involved in these shows. Dewey didn't have much respect for them anyway and he felt like it cheapened the event. I guess that's why he wasn't so fond of Agnes either."

Well, that was one of the reasons.

"What about Cecil?" I asked, thinking of the odd handshake that Dessa had mentioned seeing. "The agent. Had Dewey ever mentioned him?"

Eugene started to shake his head but stopped and frowned.

"What's wrong?" asked Granny.

"Well, Dewey had never met the agent or not that he'd told me, but something about that fellow..." He stared off into the distance. "I don't remember meeting him myself or ever hearing his name, but something seems familiar. I haven't been able to shake that feeling since last night." He blinked twice, then smiled. "But I'm sure it's nothing. I mean, he must have other clients besides Ellis. Maybe he's been to other air shows with them."

"Maybe," Hank muttered. "But if he didn't know any of these folks why did he run? And where did he go?"

Another silent stretch followed, none of us wanting to acknowledge out loud the possibility that Dewey hadn't gone anywhere of his own free will.

"I don't know about where," said Eugene, "but I can think of a reason why, a reason that isn't... you know."

A lump caught in my throat. Hope at last. "What?" I squeaked.

"Dewey was up to something," Eugene said seriously, "something he wanted to keep secret. I know Dewey. I know he wouldn't hurt anybody. But whatever it was, I'm sad to say, it was probably illegal."

"You have no idea at all what that could have been?" Hank asked.

Eugene sighed. "I'm sorry. I don't."

After that, Granny took her pictures and jotted down a little bit about Eugene's flying career. Then it was time for him to take his next passenger up, just as Miles finished with his own passenger. Granny moved over to take Miles' picture too. Hank and I moved off to a quieter spot.

"Do you think we should go ask Miles the same questions?" I asked him.

"He'll only give the same answers, I think," said Hank. I had to agree. Eugene had been the one to know Dewey best. If he didn't know—or wasn't willing to say—where Dewey was or what he'd been up to, we weren't going to do better with another round of questions.

A calling voice made us look up. A boy, maybe about twelve, ran through the long grass in his knickerbockers. "You—with the red hair!" he cried.

"Yes," answered Hank, though he rubbed the top of his head and muttered, "It's not that red."

The boy reached us, panting. "Are you Hank?" he asked.

"Yes," Hank replied again, frowning. "What's going on?"

The boy pressed a folded paper into Hank's hand. "That's for you."

Hank stared at the paper in surprise.

"Who is it from?" I asked.

"I dunno," said the boy. "All I know is I got paid a whole dime to give it to you. Read it."

The boy trotted off, ignoring my calls as Hank unfolded the paper. I gave up on the boy and turned to him. "What does it say?"

"One o'clock," Hank read, "The old barn by the cow pasture. Please come. No police. Dewey."

Chapter 8

Emmie

"What do we do?" I asked.

Hank shrugged. "I'll go to the barn, of course." He carefully refolded the paper and slipped it in his top pocket.

I rolled my eyes. "Well, obviously, but he said no police and..."

He squeezed my shoulder and gave me a sad smile that crinkled his blue eyes. "I don't like it either, but what else can we do?"

We could run to the farmhouse and ask to use the telephone to call Uncle Charlie at the station no matter what some piece of paper says.

"He must have said it for a reason," Hank insisted.

My breath caught in my chest. I wouldn't have expected Hank to act any differently, but it still vexed me. "I don't know about this."

"Emmie," he said, "do you remember last summer, the last time we got involved in a murder investigation? You trusted Dessa's opinion of someone because you trust Dessa. You were right and I was wrong. I didn't know Dessa well enough then to trust her judgment." He took my hands in his. "I hope after all these years you'd trust my judgment of people's character too."

"Of course, I trust you." I closed my eyes and thought of the boy in the tree outside my bedroom window the night before he joined the army. That was only a few years ago, though it felt like a lifetime. I thought of a younger boy who never spoke in class but caught baseballs like he was born to do it, a boy who sat on my porch and dreamed about flying machines. If Hank thought Dewey couldn't be the killer, then Dewey couldn't be the killer.

"That's not what's bothering me," I said. "Was it really Dewey who sent that note?"

"That's worrying me too." Hank rubbed the back of his neck. He pulled out the note and unfolded it again. "I never had much reason to see Dewey's handwriting during the war." A breeze blew in, ruffling my skirt and nearly blowing the paper from his hand. He hastily put it back in his pocket. "I can't say for sure he wrote this. But I also can't leave him alone in case it is him."

I nodded. No, he couldn't abandon his friend, even if it meant risking his own life. I pointed to Granny, who had finished with Miles and was heading in our direction. "She's coming over."

"Let her know I'll be back soon," said Hank, then he added, "I hope."

"What!" He was not suggesting what I thought he was. "You can't go there on your own!"

Hank clenched his fists. "Yes, I can. You don't need to get hurt."

"You need backup." I was not going to budge on this. "You at least need someone to wait near the barn and make sure you come out quickly." I checked my father's pocket watch. "We don't have much time."

"Alright," Hank said. "But what do we tell your grandmother?"

Granny was getting closer now, close enough to see we were arguing about something. She picked up the pace.

"We'll tell her the truth. I'll come with you and she can be backup. The more people who know the better. She won't like it, but I don't think she will try to stop us."

* * *

I was right. Granny neither liked it nor would she try to prevent us from going. "You two are old enough to make decisions even if I don't approve," she said. And then we began planning. Granny would wait a little distance from the old barn. I would go with Hank to the door of the barn. Hank would go in alone. If something went wrong, I could run back to tell Granny to get help, then go in and help Hank myself in whatever way I could.

Granny cast her eye about the crowded field. "If only we knew where your mothers had got to. Or your friend Dessa for that matter."

Another worrisome point. My mother and Hank's were probably busy interviewing folks, but Dessa shouldn't have taken that long talking to Agnes. I looked in the direction where they had been standing. Not a sign of either one of them.

"Maybe she's wandered off somewhere else to look for us," I said. Or maybe it hadn't been so safe sending her after the actress, but I didn't want to think about that. I pulled out my father's watch again. "We need to go. We'll be late."

We hurried away from the crowd. The oldest barn was still in line of sight for everyone at the air show, but far enough away that we would be only silhouettes in the grass. A murderer could rush out here and stab all of us in front of everyone, but no one would notice until we didn't come back in the evening. The thought made me shiver.

"You're sure it's your pilot friend who wrote that note?" asked Granny.

"I'm not sure." Hank shook his head. He stared at the barn ahead, his mouth set. "But I have to go anyway. He would go for me."

"I understand that," said Granny. "But you haven't seen him since the war. People change. And he was in a war, so perhaps he has killed people before."

Hank turned to Granny, his face pale. "I was in that war too," he said simply, then walked onward. Granny sheepishly bit her lip.

I wished I could have unheard that. *Thank you, Granny.*

When we passed the big oak tree, Granny took her leave to wait there. She checked her own watch. "It's five 'til, now. If y'all don't come back by 1:10, I'm coming in after you."

"No, Granny." This was so important. She had to understand. "You're second backup. You have to go get help if neither of us come back. If you're hurt too, there's no hope for any of us."

Granny sighed deeply. "Alright, then."

We left Granny and walked toward the barn. Another spring breeze blew through the field. On such a lovely day, it seemed impossible that we could be heading toward disaster. I almost wished it were dark and cold. The mismatch of surroundings and circumstance made me even more uneasy.

The barn appeared deserted from the outside, and for good reason. Its faded and rotting wood had seen better days. The whole structure leaned slightly and there were more than a few big holes in the sides. I suspected it had a few in the roof as well. I wondered if it was even safe for Hank to walk inside no matter who was waiting there.

"I'll be out in a moment," Hank said as we reached the door. I stood on my tiptoes and he leaned down for a kiss. Was this our last kiss? No, I couldn't let myself think that way.

"You'd better be." I hugged him close and gave him one more kiss, not caring that my grandmother was watching. I doubted she cared either. Behind us, the hole where the barn door had once been loomed, a black opening that reminded me of a hungry mouth.

"It'll be fine." He patted my shoulder. "I came out of the war okay, didn't I? I'll get through this."

"Okay," I replied. That word, *okay*, still felt odd to me to say, but it was one of the things Hank had brought back from the war, like so many other pilots, and it felt like the right word now.

Hank walked into the darkness. I watched him disappear, willing my legs to stay still, willing myself to stick to the plan like I had promised. It made more sense for us to face danger one at a time, but all I wanted to do was throw caution to the wind and run right in after him.

I hugged myself and waited. How long had it been? I pulled my father's watch from my pocket. It hadn't been a minute yet. I stared up at the towering barn. It wobbled ever so slightly in another breeze and everything creaked. This was a bad idea. I peered into the barn, shading my eyes, but I couldn't make out anything inside. I didn't hear anything either. Shouldn't Hank be talking to Dewey by now? Why didn't either of them say anything?

I rocked back and forth on my heels. *Don't be silly, Emmie,* I told myself. *They're whispering for safety. You just can't hear them.* Also, the fact that I hadn't heard anything meant that no noisy violence could have occurred. Of course, there were plenty of options for silent violence.

Then came the slightest sound. I almost thought it was the settling of the barn, but it came again. Softly, strained, a cry. "Emmie!"

I rushed in, blinking as my eyes adjusted to the darkness. A skittering sound came from somewhere. Two shapes sat on the ground. No. One crouched, the other lay still. Hank was saying something else, but something was wrong with his voice. I couldn't understand. He spoke again. This time I could make out "Watch out."

Those were the same words Dessa used the day before. My eyes finally adjusted and at last I understood. Dewey lay on the floor of the barn, limp. And Hank held him. I blinked again and noticed the dark spot on his arm, just a tiny spot. His voice came once more. "Snake."

"No!" I cried and took a step closer, but I stopped, my heart thumping so hard I thought it might burst from my chest. I had to fight my instinct. I had to turn away from the only man I'd ever loved and get Granny before I even did anything to help him.

I turned on my heel and sprinted, tears springing to my eyes and blurring everything around me. I staggered forward toward the oak tree. Toward hope.

Chapter 9

Dessa

I turned around and looked back toward where Emmie, her granny, and Hank had been standing, but they were gone. Probably they'd gone to talk with one of the other pilots. I walked in that direction, scanning the crowd as I went. Faces surrounded me. Some were neighbors I'd seen around town for years who smiled and waved. As I returned the waves, I hoped they wouldn't mention to my parents that they'd seen me here. Others were strangers. I still couldn't find my companions anywhere, but as I got closer those waiting for airplane rides, I spotted a face that was far too familiar.

My heart leapt to my throat. I turned hurriedly away from my mother. Why hadn't I borrowed a hat when I was at Emmie's house? I could have partly shielded my face with one.

I took a deep breath and focused on the grass at my feet, the cool of the earth creeping up into my shoes. *Calm down. There are lots of people here. Maybe she won't even notice you.*

A shrill voice shouted, "Odessa Child!"

No such luck.

I gathered all my courage to turn and face her again. What was done was done. At least she wasn't likely to make too much of a scene with everyone watching.

Mother stared daggers at me, her face glowing red. She opened her mouth and closed it again, clearly trying to maintain her composure. A few swift steps and I was at her side. I might as well get it over with.

"What are you doing here?" she hissed. "I don't see the sheriff anywhere."

"I—um—" I stammered, searching for a lie. A few sprang to mind. I could say Charlie was talking to Mr. McPherson and had asked me to wait here for some reason. I could say I was helping Charlie by keeping an eye on the proceedings today. But I was tired of lies. "No. He's not here," I said.

And in the middle of a crowd—an important town event, no less—what precisely could she even do about it?

"You were supposed to come straight home after helping him." She struggled to keep her furious voice to the level of a whisper. "I'll have his job for this."

I winced. She truly might. Charlie was already on thin ice, so he said. My parents weren't pleased with him to begin with, but now they might put the full power of their influence to backing whoever ran against him in the election. Probably a candidate who would take a harder stance on enforcing prohibition—except for those who could pay him well, of course. Which brought my thoughts to another matter.

"And what are you doing here, Mother?" I asked. "Aren't you supposed to be helping with some Easter event for tomorrow."

"The egg hunt for the children," Mother replied curtly. "Yes, I am."

I blinked. "That's happening on the lawn in front of town hall. Not here." That had been a big sticking point. The McPhersons had wanted to host the egg hunt too, keep things in one place, but some residents felt like an air show was too rowdy of an event for their children. Not that plenty of children hadn't shown up today and yesterday.

"Mrs.—um—Mrs. McPherson is contributing eggs. I'm here to collect them, and I thought I might as well have a look at these airplanes while I'm here." She had stammered. My mother never tripped over her words.

"You're lying." My voice was barely more than a breath. I knew what she was doing, what the McPhersons sold to those who could keep quiet.

"That's none of your concern," she said and pursed her lips.

"Really, Mother. You have no room to lecture me." I wasn't going to judge her for her own problems with alcohol, but she'd been so vocally dry, condemning the wets at every turn. It was the hypocrisy that got to me.

"I am your mother," she whispered simply. "Now, let us stop standing here in the middle of everyone and get you back home where your father and I can figure out what to do with you." She hooked one of her arms around one of mine.

I bristled. "I am not a child."

"You are behaving like a child."

"No," I shook her arm off. "I'm not." Now I was the one having trouble controlling her voice. "I am making my own choices. It's past time I did."

She leaned in close and whispered so low I could barely hear. "Why did you ask your father about money today?"

It was my turn to say, "That's none of your concern." I became aware of my heartbeat thumping in my ears. This was a dangerous conversation. I'd already ruined all the goodwill I'd gained that morning. Now I was about to ensure that my father locked up that money so tightly I'd never see it. He'd warn the bank so that I couldn't go and ask about it.

"I am done with this conversation," said Mother. "We are leaving." She took my arm again.

"Do you really want to make a scene, Mother?" I asked. I was shaking now. If everyone else at the air show hadn't been so preoccupied with the festivities, I'd already have drawn attention. "Do you want to drag me out of here? What will people say about you?"

Mother dug into my arm with her nails. I gasped. She hissed, "And what will they say about you?"

For some time, the noise around us had grown louder, but I became suddenly aware that it was not cheery chatter, but shouts and cries. I turned in the direction of the noise. Mother let go of my arm in alarm. "What's going on?" she muttered.

I heard words like "help" and "the old barn" and "snakebite." People moved in a panic, tripping on one another. "What kind of snake?" I shouted, on instinct, at no one in particular. Of course, no one replied.

Mother had gone pale. She hated snakes. "Let's go home." This time the plea sounded scared, not angry.

"You go," I told her. "I might be able to help."

"How could you...?" she began, then shook her head.

"I have to try." I squeezed her hand. Even after everything that had happened, even though I had long since known she didn't really like me, she was still my mother. Whatever that meant, it meant something. "Go home and be safe."

I ran toward the old barn—I knew the one they meant—not looking back.

Chapter 10

Emmie

It was late, long past dark, as we sat nearly silent in the parlor, drinking pot after pot of coffee. Hank was alive, a lucky break that he'd only been grazed, hadn't gotten much venom. That was all that mattered. The world had tried to take him from me, but he was still alive. Dewey had survived as well, but he was considerably worse off than Hank. The doctor thought he'd make it as well, but it was still very uncertain.

Granny rose from her chair and patted me on the arm. "The doctor said he'll be fine soon. You should sleep. We all should." Forgetting her empty coffee cup on the side table—which was not like my fastidious grandmother at all—she left the room. I listened to her footsteps as she tottered up the stairs to bed.

"She's right, you know," said Momma. "He got lucky today. We all did. We can rest knowing that." She bustled about the room, picking up the empty cups to return them to the kitchen. "Dessa, dear, you can have the spare room if you like," she called from the kitchen. "You know where it is."

Dessa could have the spare room. She could have my room. Any room she wanted as far as I was concerned and stay there forever. In the end, it was decided that I had the faster legs, and I should run for help, while Granny did what she could for Hank and Dewey. When I got back to the crowd, crying for help, who should come running but Dessa. At her instruction, we gathered ripped shirts, makeshift tools, and more from folks in the crowd. She swooped in and did what she could to help them before a doctor could be found. I could never thank her enough.

"That sounds lovely," said Dessa, rising from her seat beside me on the sofa and stretching her arms. She reached down and patted my hand. "Come on and go to sleep. You need it."

We turned out the lights and I followed her wordlessly up the stairs. I thought of Hank's parents sitting in their own house down the road. Was one of them sleeping while the other sat up with Hank? Had anyone told them to go to bed? They'd been so brave, reassuring, and cheerful when Hank talked with them croakily from his bed.

"I'll be out of here soon," Hank had told me before I left.

When we reached the landing, I asked Dessa, "What did your parents say?" When she had placed the telephone call to say she was staying here for the night, she'd been brief and I hadn't heard what was said. She'd not even asked for one of her parents to bring her clothes.

"They said goodnight," she replied, her voice suddenly high and clipped—reminding me of her mother, always icily composed in public. Then Dessa softened. "I'm sorry. I'm tired tonight. Can I talk about it later?"

"Of course," I replied. "Goodnight." We'd moved down the hall and reached our respective doors.

"Goodnight." She gave me a smile. "Hank will be just fine."

I stepped in my room and shut the door with a snap. I didn't bother with the lamp, stumbling to my bed by the light of the moon. I pulled off my shoes and pushed back the worn quilt, one Granny had made. I climbed into bed with my clothes still on and my hair still pinned up, drawing the quilt up again so it hit the bottom of my chin. I stared up at the ceiling and thought of Hank, lying sweaty in the bed, asking all of us to find the killer. I thought of Uncle Charlie, still gone, back at the station despite the late hour. My eyelids fluttered and despite the many, many cups of coffee, somehow I fell asleep.

* * *

The morning light spilled in from the window, hitting me in the face, so that as soon as I opened my eyes I squinted. What time was it? I sat up in the bed, feeling achy all over and reached for my bedside alarm clock, which I had certainly not set the night before. It was nearly eleven. I should have been in church. Blearily, I wondered why I hadn't heard Momma nagging me to get up like she usually would if I slept too late—even when we didn't have anywhere to go. Then the events of the day before flashed back. Momma hadn't tried to wake me this morning. She'd let me sleep as a kindness.

I got out of bed, dressed in clean clothes, and freshened up as best I could, then headed downstairs, following a sizzling sound into the kitchen. Granny stood before the stove, cooking. Was that...?

"Mornin', darlin'!" she cried over her shoulder. "Surprise. I got bacon the other day and I had a feeling you could use some. Happy Easter!"

"Thank you, Granny. Can I help?" I sniffed the air. Easter. Bacon. Maybe it would turn out alright.

"You don't need to do a thing. I've got it all. Just sit down at the table."

I poured myself some water and sat down as Dessa entered the kitchen, sniffing eagerly. "Did y'all have bacon?"

"We haven't had it yet." Granny turned from the stove with a grin. "But it is done now. Sit yourself down and we'll eat."

Dessa got herself a glass of water and some silverware for all of us. We ate simply right at the kitchen table. As Granny sat the sizzling plates of bacon and fried eggs—eggs!—before us, I realized how hungry I was. I hadn't even been able to think about food the night before.

"This is a wonderful Easter breakfast, Granny," I gushed between bites. "Thank you." Except it was more like "Fank you." I felt my cheeks grow warm. Momma would have scolded me for talking with my mouth full like that, but Granny didn't seem to notice.

"No trouble at all," she said and took a dainty, ladylike bite of her eggs. "I popped by to check on Hank while you were all sleeping," she said.

I fumbled my fork. "H-how is he?"

"He's doing just fine." She patted my arm. "He'll only be laid up a few days. I'm sure he'd like to see you both before you go over to the station."

"The station?" I asked. "I didn't hear Uncle Charlie come home last night and he's already back there?"

Granny shook her head. "Never did come home last night, I'm afraid. Slept in the office, he said."

I sighed and took a sip of my water. He did that sometimes when things were really bad, but it had been a long time since it was necessary.

We finished our breakfast quickly and I took the plates, but Granny snatched them out of my hands. "You let me do the washing up. It's not much for a simple breakfast. You two better get going, anyway."

We headed into the entryway where I pulled on a light sweater and Dessa grabbed the same bag she had carried all the day before.

But before we could reach the front door, it opened and Momma stepped inside, flowery Easter hat and all. "Oh, good. Y'all are awake," she said. "I'm glad you got your sleep. Church was nice today."

"Good," I replied. "Granny says Hank's doing well. We're on our way to see him before we go to the station."

Momma nodded. "Be careful in that," she jerked her head over one shoulder in the direction of where my bike was parked, "machine of yours. We don't want any more accidents."

"I will be," I said, suppressing the desire to roll my eyes. In the year and a half I'd had the motorcycle, she never had trusted either the safety of the bike itself or my capabilities as a cyclist.

Momma took off her own sweater and hung it on the hook. "I'll let y'all get going, then. Oh, and Dessa?"

Dessa looked up from where she was fiddling with her bag. "Yes, ma'am?"

"I spoke to your mother."

I couldn't imagine a conversation with Dessa's mother—who'd never been friendly with my own mother—could be anything but bad news.

Momma continued, "She's busy with the egg hunt today, but she said she'd like to speak with you soon."

"I—" Dessa began. "Oh. Is that all she said?"

"That's all she said." Momma shrugged. I was about to ask Momma how Miss Mabel—Dessa's mother—had delivered this message. Was she angry? What did that mean? But Momma checked her own watch.

"It's getting late," she said. "Better hurry."

And so we did, stepping out into another gorgeous spring day.

First, we hurried down the street on foot to Hank's house. Miss Ethel opened the door with a smile. "He's doing much better today," she said. "He's been asking after you both. Go on upstairs."

We hurried upstairs to Hank's bedroom, a bright and airy room with tall bookshelves and, near the windows, a number of houseplants which thrived whenever Hank was home from the university but otherwise barely clung to life as his mother often forgot they were even there. Hank's father, a graying version of Hank rose from his chair beside Hank's bedside when we entered. Hank, for his part sat up in bed with a book in his good hand.

"Good morning." Hank's father gave a us a smile. "We're glad to see you. And you, of course, Miss Dessa, the heroine of the hour."

Dessa flushed bright red. "I-I just did what I could do."

"Well, we're sure glad you did. I'll leave you young ones to talk a while." He yawned and stepped out into the hall. Had he slept in here? I hoped he'd gotten some rest. I took his place on the chair, grateful that none of the relatives in our lives—not Hank's parents, not my family—had reproached any of us for our actions yesterday. Whatever they thought of our decisions, there were no criticisms. Only support.

Hank sighed. "I told him he didn't need to keep sitting up here with me. I'm fine." He did look much better. Other than the dark circles under his eyes, a little pallor in his face, and the bandaged right arm, he could be perfectly normal. I wasn't sure I wanted to see under the bandage, though.

Dessa, on the other hand, bent over and peered down with professional interest.

"You really were my heroine yesterday, you know," Hank said to Dessa.

"I just helped really." She glowed red again. "Once the real doctor arrived, with real equipment, then we could really help you both."

"Any news about Dewey?" asked Hank.

I shook my head. "Not yet. We're heading to the station after this. Maybe Uncle Charlie will know something by then."

"He came by earlier this morning to interview me and he hadn't heard anything then, but it was pretty early," said Hank. "I'm surprised Charlie didn't come back to your house."

"He must be really busy," I said. "So, precisely what happened in the barn yesterday?"

Hank closed his novel. "It's a bit blurry, to be honest." He stared at the opposite wall, thinking. "I never lost consciousness—at least I don't think I did—but I suppose the shock of the whole situation made my memories fuzzy. I'll do my best to recount it."

He took a deep breath and tried to scratch his chin, but instinctively pulled up the right hand, then winced and switched to the left.

"I went into the barn and saw that Dewey was slumped over on the floor, so I hurried over to him. He had some kind of bag in his hands—or maybe a wrapped piece of cloth—that's where it gets fuzzy. I didn't smell cyanide—and I smelled it when Ellis was killed, so I knew I could smell it. Not everyone can. Right, Dessa?"

"That's right," said Dessa.

"Anyway," Hank continued, "since I didn't smell it, I thought it was safe to touch him, so I lifted him onto my lap, tried to feel for a pulse, and that's when the snake got me. I suppose it had been in the bag or maybe wrapped around his legs. It was quite dark in there. After that I called out for you, Emmie, and you went for help and…you know the rest."

I winced. I did know the rest. The moments of agony for him and for me until help could arrive.

"I remember the bag," said Dessa. "The snake was long gone. You didn't see anyone else in the barn when you and Dewey were there alone?" asked Dessa. "You didn't hear anyone?"

"I'm afraid not," said Hank. "I heard a rustling sound that later turned out to be the snake. But I didn't hear or see any people besides Dewey. I suppose if someone else had been there, they'd already left. Or they were very quiet."

"This whole thing is bizarre," I said. "What was he doing in the barn? Why did he hide and why did he ask you to come?"

"I have no idea," said Hank. "Even if he were the murderer, surely he would have run away, not hidden off in a barn full of snakes."

Dessa held her head in her hands. "I have more to tell you all from yesterday."

She proceeded to explain what Agnes had said to her.

"So, the killer might not be in Georgia at all!" I exclaimed.

"So Agnes says," said Dessa in a dark tone. "But we only have her word for that."

"And she was with Ellis—and that odd flag in a bag—the whole time," Hank said, nodding.

"She's our prime suspect." I rose from the chair. "And Dewey's hiding was just a distraction. We'd better get to the station and talk to Uncle Charlie."

"Yes, you had better," Hank agreed. "I wish I was coming with you, but go solve that murder for me."

I laughed and Hank laughed too. "We'll try," I said.

We hurried back to my house. I pinned my skirt in place and we hopped on the motorcycle, Dessa in the sidecar. We sped through the still-bustling town. Not even a murder and two snakebites could deter the Easter celebration. We passed through downtown on the way to the station, driving right by the egg hunt. In front of town hall, children searched under bushes and flowers, squealing as they pulled out brightly colored eggs. "Your mother was helping with the egg hunt right?" I asked Dessa, letting all the questions I wanted to ask lay unsaid.

Dessa took my meaning. "Yes, she did. Yesterday, we... Well, she saw me at the air show." And so the whole story spilled out, her asking after the money at breakfast the day before, their argument at the air show which only ended when Hank was bitten by the snake, the terse telephone conversation that followed when we finally got back to my house. "And so I think I've spoiled it all," she said. "I'll never get the money now. I'll never persuade them to let me go to the university. I'll be lucky if they don't stop me from going back to Lucy Cobb, even though tuition's already paid." She sat with her head drooped against the side of the sidecar. I'd never seen her cry—not even under the toughest circumstances last summer, but I thought she might actually be close to tears now.

I wished I could comfort her better, give her hug, but I needed both hands firmly on the handlebars. "I'm sure you haven't ruined everything," I said in as sensible-sounding a voice as I could manage. "Besides," and this was true, "they're not likely to remove you from school when you've got stellar grades and there's only two months until graduation. It's much less fuss and less awkward to simply let you finish."

That seemed to make her feel a little better.

In a few minutes, we had pulled up outside the station. We hurried inside. Uncle Charlie slouched in his desk chair, papers in one hand, coffee cup in the other.

"Morning," he said in a hoarse voice. "Set on down. Let's catch each other up."

We told him everything we'd learned, everything that had happened since we'd last been able to speak. He nodded and took notes, slurping noisily from the cup."

"That's good. Very good to know," he said simply when we were done. Even he hadn't chastised me for letting Hank meet Dewey in the barn. I almost wanted someone to so I wouldn't keep berating myself in my own head. If only I'd stopped him...

But then, if I'd stopped him, Dewey might be dead. The snake could have struck again or even if we'd stopped to get help before going to the barn, we might not have found him in time.

"Have you heard about how Dewey is doing?" I asked.

"He's awake this morning, apparently," said Uncle Charlie. "I'll go see him in a few minutes if you two want to come."

I absolutely stared at my uncle, right into his dark-circled eyes. "Really? You want us to come?" What happened to wanting us to be discreet?

He set down his cup with a clatter and ran one hand over his tired face. "Might as well. I really shouldn't have asked you to back off because of my job. That was a selfish motivation and I'm going to lose the next election anyway."

I opened my mouth to protest—to tell him we'd canvass day and night to make sure he won, but he didn't let me even get started.

"I'm not saying I won't try, but I know the odds. There are a lot of folks who don't like how I've done things. I've tried my whole life to uphold the spirit of the law, the ideas of justice, and I'm not saying I've done it perfectly—far from it, but... I'm getting distracted here. The point is my ideas of what's

64

important have always been too progressive for some in this town and those voices are growing louder." He sighed. "Let's not worry about that too much today. We've got a murder to solve. If I take you two along on this interview, I might get to the bottom of it faster." His eyes twinkled. "And it would keep you much safer than if you just went off on your own."

The three of us hurried over on foot to the doctor's house, where Dewey was staying. He could hardly have been sent back to the bed and breakfast where he'd been staying before the snakebite. On the way, Uncle Charlie filled us in on a few details. Agnes had indeed inherited all of Ellis' fortune, giving her a strong motive. After many telephone calls to California, he'd not been able to find anyone who had seen Ellis pack the fateful bag he took on his trip.

"What about the train trip he was supposed to make?" asked Dessa. "Does that factor into this at all?"

"Perhaps," said Uncle Charlie, stroking his mustache. "But if so, I don't yet know how. It's quite possible it really was merely a publicity stunt on Ellis and Agnes' part. Agnes said as much—as much as we want to trust her word on the matter, that is."

"And what about Cecil?" I asked. "And Dewey was up to something, everyone thinks so." And that wasn't even touching the possibility that Cecil had raised about there being a hired killer involved—although, given what we now knew about how the bag had traveled, it seemed unlikely to me. Why would Agnes hire someone to place poison in a bag that had been literally at her side for many hours?

"I have a hunch about both of those things," said Uncle Charlie. "When I talk to Dewey, perhaps we'll see if I'm right."

When we arrived at the doctor's house, the doctor greeted us brightly.

"Nice to see you again, Doc," he said to Dessa, and she blushed and stammered in response.

Dewey was in the spare bedroom the doctor used for the worst cases and those who couldn't be sent home for some reason. Darkly, I wondered what had happened to the remains of the worst-off patient he'd seen in some time—Ellis. He couldn't be being stored around here somewhere, surely. No, he was probably sent to off to Athens to the morgue. I shivered. *Think about the present and what's in front of you, Emmie. No sense pondering that.*

Dewey pushed him up on his pillows. His face was ashen, and he shook slightly. He'd clearly been much more affected than Hank had, had a bigger dose of venom, but not a fatal one. "Nice to see you all." He gave a wan smile. "How's Hank doing? I heard he got bit too."

"Doing just fine," said Uncle Charlie. "We all talked to him this morning. He was ready to leap out of bed and help me keep investigating if I had let him."

Dewey chuckled faintly. "That sounds like Hank. Good to hear." He lowered himself again. "I hope you don't mind if I lay down while we talk."

"Not at all," said Uncle Charlie. "Do what you need to do."

"Thank you so much, little Doc," Dewey said in a croaky voice, lifting one hand in Dessa's direction. "I heard what you did for me—for both of us."

"It—I—" she stammered and reddened.

Uncle Charlie cleared his throat. "Now you're able to hold a conversation, I do have some questions to ask."

"Of course," said Dewey. He closed his eyes but said. "I'm still awake. I'm listening."

"Let's start with Cecil," Uncle Charlie began. "Are you sure you never met him before this air show?"

Dewey surprised me by saying, "I might as well come clean about the whole thing. We were running cocaine."

Cocaine! I bit my lip to stop myself crying out, *What!* Dessa's eyes widened.

"So, the white powder we saw…" I began.

"No, no. That was powdered cyanide," Uncle Charlie said. "Like Dessa, I could tell at once from the scent once Ellis made contact and his bodily fluids wetted the powder. But the tricky part is, if Cecil was the killer and was also running cocaine, anyone in on his dealing wouldn't have been at all surprised to see him carrying white powder, if they had found it. He'd have had to be very careful with labeling, though, to make sure he could tell them apart."

"That's right," croaked Dewey. "I suspected Ellis was involved too. The bag switch was part of the deal. He brought one bag, stuffed with cocaine…"

"That's why he never let it leave his side," said Dessa.

"...and then Cecil would switch it for an identical bag with the flag in it..."

"...which he'd stuffed inside that big, clunky briefcase," I said.

"But the bag he switched out was laced with cyanide," said Uncle Charlie.

"And Cecil would have had to stow the cocaine somewhere after the murder," said Dessa. "The old barn."

"He's our killer!" I cried.

Uncle Charlie raised one hand. "Perhaps. Dewey, are you sure Ellis switched the bags? Did you see him?"

"Just my guess," said Dewey.

Darn. That didn't rule out Agnes, then. Or some mysterious other person back in California.

"Did you confront Cecil about this?" asked Uncle Charlie.

"I did," said Dewey. "I told him I'd turn him in if he'd didn't come clean. It wasn't easy. Well, it's all out now and I'm in for it for running cocaine myself. But I was willing to go to jail if meant catching a murderer."

"Why did you hide?" I asked.

"I panicked," said Dewey. "I thought I could cover things up if I just had time. I wasn't really hiding, I just didn't go back to my hotel, trying to get rid of what I had stashed on me before the police found it. I was so worried I didn't think about how it looked until later."

"What did Cecil say when you confronted him?" asked Uncle Charlie.

"He brushed it off, but he sent me a note to meet him in the old barn. I hoped he'd explain himself." Another note.

"Was he there when you arrived?" asked Uncle Charlie.

"No," said Dewey. "Not that I could see in the dark anyway. All I found was a bag on the ground—like any drop-off. I opened it and found... Well, you know what I found."

I turned to Uncle Charlie. "Was there cocaine in the bag as well?"

He shook his head. "Nothing but a snake."

"Why did you send for Hank to come see you?" I asked.

"I didn't," said Dewey, his eyes flying open. "I thought he'd just happened to find me and been bitten too. I didn't know he thought I'd sent for him."

"He got a note too," I said. "Telling him to meet at the barn, supposedly from you."

Dewey passed his good hand over his face. "I've made such a mess of things. A man is dead, I'm lying here laid up, I'll be going to jail, and my buddy's been bitten by a snake that was meant for me."

"Meant for you?" I asked. "What do you mean?"

Dewey propped himself upright again. "This was no accident. I told you I found the snake in the bag, but it was latched shut. The snake's not likely to have crawled in on its own. Someone put it there. Cecil put it there."

"You're sure it was Cecil?" asked Uncle Charlie. "Does he have experience handling snakes?" Indeed, if most folks tried to pick up and move a rattlesnake, they'd be bitten for certain.

"Maybe not." Dewey frowned. "But who else could it be? Who else would know the drop off spot? It's not like anyone else has experience with…" A pained look crossed his face.

"What's wrong?" asked Dessa. "Are you in more pain?"

Dewey shook his head. "I've just remembered. Agnes' last film. *The Snake Charmer.* She does all her own stunt work, doesn't she?"

Chapter 11

Emmie

We headed to talk to Agnes after a few quick telephone calls in which Uncle Charlie confirmed that Agnes was still at the bed and breakfast where she had been staying. Cecil, however, had disappeared, adding to the confusion.

"Now, he may have run off simply because of the cocaine dealing, nothing to do with the murder," said Uncle Charlie. It still made me wary of Cecil, though.

The bed and breakfast was only two blocks away, but we went back to the station and took Uncle Charlie's police car, just in case some new information meant an arrest.

The bed and breakfast itself was a quaint little house. I'd naturally never needed to stay there myself, but they had a large music room that my piano teacher had used years ago for our twice-a-year recitals. When I stepped in the door and glimpsed the piano through an open door, my hands automatically flexed, even though it had been ages since I played anything. Not after the teachers at The Lucy Cobb Institute decided my taste in music was "too modern." Their loss.

Agnes waited for us at a window-side table in the breakfast room. She tossed her hair lazily and did not rise as we entered. I supposed she was used to people doing that for her, not the other way around. She took a drag of her cigarette. "How can I help?" she asked with one raised eyebrow and in a tone that said clearly that she hoped this would be quick.

We took seats at the table without waiting to be asked. Uncle Charlie began:

"What do you know about Ellis Singleton and cocaine?"

She gave a hollow laugh. "I wondered when that nasty business would come up. What do I know? I know he enjoyed it quite a bit."

Uncle Charlie was unfazed. "What do you know about Ellis and *running* cocaine?"

She blinked. "He did that from time to time, yes. Did I approve of it? No. But my approval or disapproval never stopped my fiancé from doing anything he set his mind to." She tapped her cigarette on the ashtray. My nose twitched. Uncle Charlie smoked—sometimes cigarettes, sometimes cigars—every day of his life, but Momma would have had her own twin brother's hide if he'd done so inside of the house, let alone in a hotel, a place that didn't even belong to us. It was becoming more and more common, though, even for ladies, to smoke in any room of any house—not just a gentleman's parlor or smoking room, but Momma's manners had rubbed off on me. I wasn't fond of this particular modernization.

Dessa spoke up now, startling me. "Why did Ellis run cocaine, though?" she asked. "Surely he was paid well enough for his acting?"

Agnes sneered in Dessa's direction. "That's right, doctor girl. He was a big earner and a big spender. In debt up to his eyeballs. That inheritance everyone thinks I murdered him for? Nothing but a pile of bills."

"If you'll forgive my saying so," said Dessa with an edge to her voice I'd never heard before, "it didn't seem like you and your fiancé actually got along very well."

Agnes blew smoke right into Dessa's face. Dessa coughed and wiped away water from her eyes. "I do mind your saying," said Agnes, her voice honeyed, "but, no, we did not get along very well. When our studio set up the courtship and engagement, they didn't take into account personality, only what our combined fame could gain for them."

To my surprise, Dessa didn't shy away, but resumed staring daggers at her with bloodshot eyes. "And you both agreed to this arrangement?"

Agnes shrugged. "There was money to be made. I would have been alright with simply ignoring his infidelities—which were numerous—and turning a mostly blind eye to the cocaine, as long as he wasn't putting me at risk.

No, the real problem with our planned union was Ellis' desire to constantly upstage me. He could never bear to have all eyes in the room anywhere but on him. Even that stupid flag stunt at the barnstormer was something he stole from one of my films, not his. I waved it at the start of a motorcar race."

I pounced on what she'd let slip there. "So, he wasn't a threat to you when he was simply using cocaine, but when he was carrying it places, distributing it, that put your career at risk, didn't it?"

"Of course, it did," she spat. "It's illegal. And not like how booze is illegal but everybody does it anyway. He was going to get caught someday. He was playing with jail time or worse. And I didn't want to be caught in the middle. I suppose I am now, aren't I?"

I held off pointing out that Ellis had gotten in rather more trouble than anyone else, being now dead.

"So, if I go upstairs right now," said Uncle Charlie, "and look through your room, I won't find any cocaine among your possessions?"

Agnes raised her voice. "No. You won't." She slammed a fist on the table. The ashtray clinked against the wood. "Go up there right now for all I care. Go look. I have nothing to hide. No cocaine. No cyanide."

Uncle Charlie rose from the table. "I will go look, thank you." Dessa and I rose as well. "One other thing," said Uncle Charlie. "You were in a film called *The Snake Charmer.* Is that correct?"

This time she slammed down her fist so hard, the ashtray skittered to the edge of the table. "Now I put a snake on that pilot, did I? I did star in a moving picture called *The Snake Charmer.* An excellent film, by the way. No one wants to talk about that. But I held garter snakes with wax bits stuck to either side of them to make them look like cobras. They weren't even pretending to be rattlesnakes, which is what bit the pilot, isn't it? The snakes I held were completely harmless. It's a movie! Why on earth would we use real poisonous snakes?"

Uncle Charlie nodded and headed toward the stairs, Dessa following. I hung back. Of course, she could be lying, but if Agnes were telling the truth, I felt a little sorry for her. She had been paired with an unsuitable match who actively upstaged her. Then he'd been killed rather horribly in her presence,

71

leaving her to deal with his creditors. Finally, here we were almost accusing her of his murder.

"I know it's been awful for you," I began.

"It's been horrible." She turned away from me and faced the window. "I can't wait until that stupid sheriff of yours lets me leave this place so I can never have to look at it again."

"If it helps, while you're stuck here, we could do a photo shoot for the paper." I thought she might like a moment in the spotlight, just her. "All about you. Not about the investigation."

"Are you kidding me!" Agnes roared. She spun around in her chair, a ferocious look on her face. "I wouldn't use your pathetic excuse for a newspaper to wipe…"

She went on, but I don't care to repeat what she said.

Chapter 12

Emmie

Later that afternoon, we were back at home. Dessa and Uncle Charlie's search of Agnes' room had turned up no new evidence. As she had said, she had nothing to hide. Whether that was because nothing was ever there or because she had disposed of it, who was to say? Given the circumstances, Cecil was now the prime suspect, so there was little for us to do but wait for the police—either here or in the surrounding counties—to discover him.

Momma and Dessa were in the kitchen, cooking us rather more Easter supper than five people could eat, while Granny had a special task for me. "Come in here." She beckoned me from the doorway of her bedroom with one finger. "I need some help."

I followed her in to find her cozy bedroom and sitting nook transformed. She'd not only drawn the curtains but done something more to lower the light. How else could it be that dark in the middle of a sunny day? "Did you paper the windows?" I asked.

"I certainly did," she said. "Look here."

Granny had pushed two desks together in her sitting nook, and those she had made her workstation. There were basins that gave off a smell that reminded me of chemistry class and stacks of materials. The whole area—desks, floor, and all—was covered in old newspaper to catch drips. She'd rigged up a clothesline between two lamps. "It's time to develop our pictures," she said.

I followed her directions and watched the magic as images sprang to life on the paper. It was such a strange and complicated setup, it almost felt like it shouldn't work at all, even though she explained the chemical process as we worked. It still seemed like a miracle to me each time a new image appeared.

I hung up the developing photograph of Eugene standing by his plane. It was a shame we couldn't get one of Agnes and her plane, but I supposed I shouldn't have been too surprised she'd refused. At least Eugene's plane looked very like Agnes'. The same model, I thought. Only the pilot would have been different.

"This is such fun, Granny," I said. "So, you said earlier my father was a journalist. Momma never told me that."

"Oh, yes," said Granny, hanging up another photograph. "When we met him, he was a reporter. He had such a sense of adventure. Something he certainly passed on to you." In the dim light, I could see her eyes twinkle. "I wish your momma would speak more about him to you, but I know why she doesn't. She was so—" Granny paused. "Despondent is the only word that comes to mind. I'd never seen anyone as miserable before, after your father died. And he was so young too. Only a few years older than you are now. With you just a little baby. It was tragic, really, he had such a drive to do things, to do good in the world. But he barely had a chance."

My hands shook as I dipped the paper, and I realized my heart was racing. It was so unfair. Whenever I thought of my father, that's what came to mind. It was so unfair he was taken so soon. A small injury that led to a fever and then suddenly he was gone. He never got to see me grow up. I never got to know him. I didn't even remember him.

"Momma has tried to do that good for him, hasn't she," I said, blinking away tears.

"She sure has," Granny said, her voice bursting with pride. "She's spent her whole life working for one cause or another. Life may not be fair, but that's not for lack of trying on your mother's part."

If only one day my mother could talk about me in that tone. But despite hurrying through my basic curriculum, I'd flitted from thing to thing, looking for adventure. Had I done anything to be proud of? Could I ever be someone to be proud of? I looked at the photographs hanging on the line. If journalism was right for my father, maybe it would be right for me too. There were plenty who made up stories, printed lies just to sell, but there was also a lot of good to be done by shining a light on the truth. And yes, travel and adventure too. Having the university education would be helpful, but I didn't need it to be a reporter or a photographer.

"I've been thinking," I said, my hands shaking worse now, "about what I might do with my life if I don't get into a university." And, honestly, maybe I still would pursue journalism even if I got the degree.

In a wavering voice, I told Granny everything, how I'd wondered if I had even a chance to get into The University of Georgia or any four-year school. I told her how I only wanted to do something meaningful, to be someone that she and Momma and Uncle Charlie could be proud of. I wanted to be someone my father could have been proud of too.

"Oh, my darling!" Granny's voice broke. "We are proud of you. The you that's right now. Look at what you've done and who you are. You are a bright, adventurous young woman who's never afraid of a challenge. No matter what you do with your life, we will always be proud of you."

I sniffed. I felt lighter, and I was also certain I was about to cry in the most undignified way.

We dropped our tools, heedless of the mess, and hugged each other tight right then and there.

Chapter 13

Dessa

I rushed from the kitchen to answer a knock at the door. A woman with gray-streaked, dark hair who I'd never seen before stood on the porch, several suitcases at her feet. Were Emmie's family expecting visitors? "Hello," I said. "How can I help?"

"You must be Dessa." The woman smiled, deepening the crinkles at the corners of her eyes. "You look just like your mother. I know I haven't seen you in many, many years, so I don't expect you to remember me. I'm your Aunt Margaret. Can I come inside?"

Aunt Margaret. I'd forgotten I was supposed to be home in time for her arrival until well into the previous evening. And then, with everything going on, I'd barely given her a thought afterward. My shoulders stiffened. I looked from side to side. Aunt Margaret had arrived alone, apparently having carried these cases on foot. What was happening here?

"Of course," I said. "Let me take your things."

"Actually," Aunt Margaret said in a strained voice, "these are your things. When I said I was coming to see you, your father asked me to bring them along."

So that was that, then. I blinked. Connection severed. I wasn't going back. "Oh. Alright." I brought the cases into the hall automatically, following Aunt Margaret inside like a stiff machine. I felt odd, like I was floating slightly outside of myself. All those years and now, done. Gone. I'd left. I wasn't sure if I was relieved or upset. I closed the front door behind us.

Emmie's mother had come out into the entryway now. "Hello," she said warily.

"This is my Aunt Margaret," I explained. My voice sounded like it was coming from someone else, not me. "She brought me my things."

Emmie's mother relaxed. "That was kind. Welcome, Margaret. I'm sure you'd like to have chat with your niece. I can make some tea or coffee, if you like."

"That would be lovely," said Aunt Margaret in a soft tone that sounded like genuine appreciation. "Thank you." Emmie's mother popped back into the kitchen.

"Let me show you to the parlor," I said and led the way.

We settled ourselves in the comfortable wingback chairs. I took a deep, shaky breath. "I'm sorry I wasn't there to meet you when you arrived."

"That's alright," said Aunt Margaret with a smile. "I heard about what happened at the farm. I understand that you were quite busy"

I stifled a laugh at the understatement.

"You're probably wondering what to make of me," said Aunt Margaret. "I understand some falling out has occurred between you and your parents, and I am a relative stranger—to you at least—maybe to my own brother as well. Over ten years of absence can do that. I just came today because I wanted a chance to see my only niece and perhaps hear her side of the story." She paused, then added quickly, "If you are willing and ready to tell, that is. I have no right to compel you, and you have no real reason to trust me."

I opened my mouth, which was feeling suddenly dry, then closed it again. What if this was a trick? What if she was getting information to feed back to my parents who would then...do what? I sat up straight in my chair. I felt bolder, stronger than I had perhaps ever felt. What could they do anyway? I was no longer afraid they'd pack me off to sanitarium. It was far easier with fewer messy questions to answer to send me somewhere more pleasant, like the boarding school where they actually had sent me. I was no longer afraid they would boot me from the house, since the suitcases in the entryway meant they already had. If they couldn't marry me off to someone politically expedient for them, it was simpler to just let me go. All of the things I'd been afraid they'd do weren't real threats at all. My parents had never had the power I had imagined they did.

And now I had one actual relative sitting before me, offering her own olive branch. I decided to take it.

I told Aunt Margaret nearly everything, even the things I'd hidden from my parents, like the girlfriends and the application to the university. She nodded and listened. At some point, Emmie's mother brought in tea. I was barely paying attention to my surroundings. When I finished, I drank the cold tea that sat on the table next to me. Aunt Margaret did the same. The silence stretched on, punctuated by the ticking of the grandfather clock in the hallway and the sound of twittering birds through the open window. What was she thinking?

"I can see why you might choose to live apart from your parents," she said finally. "I don't imagine it's been very pleasant for you."

I nodded. I wasn't sure if this was acceptance, but it wasn't rejection at least.

Aunt Margaret continued, "I understand you asked your father yesterday about your inheritance. Were you hoping to use that for tuition?"

"Yes," I replied. "Or for a fresh start somewhere else if I don't get into the university. But I don't need it." And I didn't, I realized at last. If I was clever enough to get into the university, I could be clever enough to find a way to pay for it. And if I didn't get in, then I'd get a job and make my own way. In the meantime, I had friends who could help me get on my feet.

"All the same, let me see what I can do about that," she said. "Your granddad meant that money for you. I'm sure he would want you to have it." She reached over and patted my knee. "Thank you for telling me all this. I think you've made some fine choices, Dessa. And I know your relationship with your parents may be broken, but I do hope that we can be friends."

My cup shook in my hands, and I hastily replaced it on the table. "That—that would be lovely," I said. "Would you like to stay for supper?"

Chapter 14

Emmie

After we finished upstairs, Granny and I went into the kitchen with Momma, and let Dessa and her aunt have some privacy in the parlor. Another knock at the door brought me out of the kitchen, however. I was surprised to find Eugene on the front porch, hat in hand.

"Happy Easter," he said with a smile. "I hoped I'd gone to the right house. I've just been to talk with Dewey and the doctor told me where you were."

"Happy Easter to you too," I said. "Come inside."

Eugene wiped his boots and stepped in. "I was coming to thank you and your friend for helping Dewey yesterday. The air show can't go on, naturally, but I'd like to offer you both a ride in my plane this afternoon."

A ride in the plane. A chill ran through my whole body. With a murder and two snakebites, I'd thought I'd steered clear of any possible airplane rides. I was struggling to find an excuse, when Dessa and the woman I presumed was her aunt popped into view.

"That would be lovely!" Dessa cried. "See, Emmie, we haven't missed out after all."

"Yes." My voice came out high-pitched and strange. Lovely.

Dessa turned to her aunt. "Oh, but I can't leave you here. How rude of me. Unless you'd like to come along?"

Her aunt nodded eagerly. "I'd love to come watch." Great.

An excuse struck me like a bolt of lightning. "Oh, but Momma may need us to help cook."

Momma and Granny popped into the entryway now. "You can't pass up an opportunity like this," said Momma, "and such a kind offer too. We don't need any help. We'll keep everything warm for when you all come back."

I swallowed, my last hope gone. I squeaked out assent using that pilot word of Hank's, "Okay."

* * *

Eugene had borrowed a car, so it was only a few minutes until we were back at the McPhersons' farm, hiking over to the shiny airplane.

"It's beautiful," cried Dessa's Aunt Margaret. "I'm so disappointed I never got to see the actual air show."

Eugene winked at her. "After the rides, maybe I'll do a few tricks for you."

I gently nudged Dessa forward. "You should go first. You're the one who really saved the day, Doc."

She stood on her tiptoes and eyed the airplane eagerly. "Oh, but I couldn't," she said. "You've had to hear about air travel nonstop from Hank for years. It's time you finally got a chance to experience it yourself." Now she nudged me forward. I thought for a moment about simply running all the way back to the house, but Eugene was already preparing for flight. I wasn't going to get out of this, so perhaps it was best to go first and get it over with.

I followed Eugene's directions in climbing into the passenger seat. "No worries," he said. "I've got two parachutes. Not that we'll need them, of course." He laughed.

"Of course," I repeated numbly. This was simply another scary situation like so many I had been in before. The trick was thinking only one step at a time. Get in the airplane. Don't think about the fact that you are about to go up, up, up, higher than humans are supposed to go. I hugged the parachute pack.

In a few moments, Eugene had the machine roaring to life. He checked some details—I don't know what—and we were ready faster than I really would have preferred. I thought about closing my eyes, but I decided not seeing would actually make this more terrifying.

Eugene shouted out various pieces of information about the airplane or what he was doing, but I could barely hear over the noise and barely pay any attention while I tried to keep myself focused on staying very firmly in my seat. Why did these things have an open top? I thought I caught the words "wing" and "engine" and "propeller." As long as they were all in working order, I hardly cared what he was up to.

Soon the plane moved forward, faster and faster and before I was ready I felt a lightness as the wheels lifted from the ground. And we were off, up into the sky, higher and higher in this tin can with wings. *You did it,* I told myself. *You sat down in this death trap, and now he can fly around a minute and then you can get back on the nice, safe earth.*

The wind whipped at us and I clung to the parachute pack more firmly. "Isn't gorgeous up here!" I heard Eugene cry over the noise of the wind and the engine. "Flying like birds, the two of us, in a contraption only invented in 1903."

Don't remind me. The airplane as a device was younger than I was, and yet it was dangling me far above the trees. Or so I thought. I'd not yet let myself look outside my seat.

Get a hold of yourself, Emmie. When will you have a chance to ride in an airplane again? I forced myself to peer very carefully over my shoulder. The world lay far below me, small and strange-looking. So, this was what the birds saw, what Hank had seen every time he went up in a plane during the war. For a second, over my internal alarm, I appreciated the beauty and exhilaration. No wonder Hank loved this so much.

Eugene was talking again. I caught the word "Uh-oh" over the noise. "Uh-oh?" I asked, my stomach dropping. "What's uh-oh?"

"Nothing, nothing!" Eugene shouted back. Then I noticed the slight shaking sensation I'd experienced throughout the short flight was growing stronger.

"Are you sure it's nothing?" I shouted back.

In front of me, Eugene's arms and hands moved. I supposed he was fiddling with the controls. I peered down once more. Were the trees getting larger? Was the ground getting closer?

"Are we supposed to be going down?" I cried, my breath coming in shallow gasps. *Okay.* I repeated the word in mind. *It's okay. Okay.*

"No!" he cried back. He said some more words I couldn't quite catch, but I heard "engine" a few times and "I checked this morning" and "sabotage."

My internal alarm was at full blast now. Sabotage? The murders weren't over. But how? Why? What did Eugene do to anyone? The ground was definitely closer now.

I heard Eugene say "parachute" very clearly. No. No-no-no-no. That was impossible. I was frozen to the seat. The only thing worse than being stuck in a falling plane would be leaping out of one.

Eugene was wiggling around, clearly struggling. "I can't keep this up for long. You have to go!"

I slid the parachute pack around my shoulders. There was no way I could do this.

"Jump and pull the cord!" he shouted.

I had to do this. *Don't think, Emmie, just go.* I found the cord with one hand, held tight to the arm straps of the pack with the other, and rose from my seat. *I can't be doing this. I can't be doing this.*

"Jump now!" shouted Eugene.

I jumped.

The sky was so blue, dotted with bright white clouds. And the ground was so green rushing to meet me. All I could let myself think of were the bright, bright colors. That and pulling the cord. I pulled. All the weight of gravity hit me as the bright white parachute erupted above me. My descent slowed, and the earth approached at much more gentle speed now. One much less likely to break bones.

I gently landed on the safe, green earth and tumbled, shaking, but alright to the ground. I looked to the sky. Eugene in his own parachute was sailing gently down about a hundred yards away from me. In the distance I saw the beautiful plane, so like Agnes' plane, crash and catch fire, the flames destroying the gorgeous paintwork.

And there it was, the missing motive. Cecil had never intended to kill Ellis in the first place. The poison was meant for Agnes. She was the one causing problems, complaining about the cocaine scheme. Maybe Ellis really was going to stop. Maybe Agnes was going to turn Cecil in. The flag was from Agnes' movie, not one of Ellis' films. Cecil probably thought she'd be waving it. But Ellis had upstaged her, refused to let her share the limelight. And it had been the last thing he'd ever done.

Chapter 15

Emmie

Easter Monday was a relaxed affair. According to the police, all signs pointed to Cecil being in a neighboring county, so tired Uncle Charlie finally got a day to rest at home.

"Not my jurisdiction," he said ruefully, raising his glass of tea.

"Maybe someone will catch him soon," I said.

A knock brought me to the door. I opened it to find Hank and Miss Ethel on the porch.

"You're here!" I cried, fighting the urge to jump into his arms. He could hardly catch me in his state.

"I felt up to a short walk today." Hank shrugged.

Miss Ethel smiled. "He thought he might come over here and eat your food."

I stepped aside and let them in. "You two can come sit in our parlor and eat our food all day if you want."

They entered the parlor to cheers from Uncle Charlie, Dessa, and Granny. In the back of the house, the telephone rang out. Momma entered the parlor a few moments later.

"Charlie! They caught him!" she cried. Then blinked at the full room. "Oh, hello, Ethel, Hank."

Charlie sat up straight. "Where'd they find him."

"Tried to board a train," said Momma. "Using a false name, but the pho-tographs had gotten around. The stationmaster recognized him. Apparently, he'd switched out that battered briefcase for some other piece of luggage, but it was absolutely stuffed with cocaine."

"Well, they've got him on that charge at least," said Uncle Charlie. "With any luck, my deputies will have enough evidence to charge him with murder too. I should really be out there with them."

Momma wagged a finger. "No, you shouldn't! They've got this handled. You take your much-needed break. You should really be napping today." She hurried off again, probably to get biscuits and coffee. Uncle Charlie grumbled and sat back in his seat.

"What I don't understand," said Hank, easing himself into a comfortable wingback chair, "is how Cecil managed to plant the snake for Dewey."

"That was interesting." Uncle Charlie leaned forward. "At first, I really thought Dewey must have been mistaken or misremembering. After all, when we first met him, Cecil seemed so clueless about nature and life in the country. I remember you all said he bit into a papier-mâché apple."

Hank, Dessa, and I chuckled. "I could barely believe anyone could be so foolish," I said.

"Wouldn't he have felt that it wasn't real when he picked it up?" asked Dessa.

"That's exactly right," said Uncle Charlie. "And eventually it made me suspicious. No one is that stupid. It was an act. A few telephone calls to California revealed that years before he'd become an agent, he took part in wild west shows." Uncle Charlie paused for effect. "His most popular act, apparently, was the rattlesnake roundup."

"So, he knew how to handle them," I said. "And the woods around the McPhersons' farm is full of snakes. They wouldn't have been too hard to find for someone who knows snakes well."

"Exactly," Cecil said. "He was somewhat cleverer than we realized, but his mistake was misjudging Dewey's character. Dewey wasn't willing to cover a murder to save his own skin. That's what made the plans fall apart. And when Dewey and you survived the snakebite, he sabotaged the wrong plane and ran."

We sat in silence a moment, each of us appreciating how close we'd come to disaster and how Ellis had not escaped it.

Momma bustled into the parlor with a tea tray laden down with snacks, tea, and cups. And something else as well: the mail.

She set down the tray on a side table. "This looks important, Emmie, dear." She handed me an envelope with my name on it, a letter forwarded from school, a letter from The University of Georgia.

I took it with trembling hands.

"We're proud of you no matter what it says," said Granny.

"And even if you get in and decide you don't want to go," added Momma.

But I did want to go. I truly did. "I know I'm not cut out to be a doctor like Dessa's going to be," I said, "or a lawyer like Hank's going to be." Hank mumbled something and rubbed the back of his neck with his good hand.

"You'll be wonderful," said Momma, "whatever you become."

I held my breath and ripped open the envelope. I unfolded the paper within.

The words seemed to jumble before my eyes, but I read one line quite clearly: "We are pleased to offer you a place in the class of 1922."

"I did it!" I cried in a squeaky voice I barely recognized as my own. "I'm going to get a bachelor's degree!" Cheers erupted all around.

"I should've gotten more bacon!" cried Granny.

* * *

Dessa

As we celebrated Emmie's acceptance, someone rapped on the front door. Being the non-relation in the room, I hurried to get it and let them continue congratulating her.

Aunt Margaret waited on the step. "I can tell that some good news has reached this house," she said with smile, leaning toward the sound coming from the direction of the parlor.

"Yes," I said, a little breathless. "Emmie's going to the university next year."

"That's wonderful," said Aunt Margaret. "The postman comes to your father's house before this one, I gather. I've got something for you as well." She held out an envelope.

I thought about rushing back in to share with the others, but what if I wasn't so lucky? Did I want them to see my disappointment? No. Best to compose myself here on the porch. I stepped out, closing the door behind me, and took the envelope.

"Would you prefer if I left?" asked Aunt Margaret.

I looked up into her blue eyes, the same speckled blue as my father's, but I saw no judgment there. "No," I said. "Please stay." Maybe it would be nice to have one other person with me when I learned the news. I opened the envelope and read the contents.

I looked up into those blue eyes. "I got in."

Get a Free Story

More Emmie and Dessa adventures are coming soon. In the meantime, do you wonder what Emmie's Uncle Charlie got up to before he was a sheriff? Back in 1900, when he and Emmie's mother were teenagers, they had their own mystery adventure. This short story is available exclusively to folks subscribed to Connie B. Dowell's newsletter.

At the turn of the twentieth century, a massive theft puts a town in jeopardy. Eighteen-year-old Charlie wants to set things right.

In this prequel to the Emmie and Dessa Mysteries, follow Emmie's Uncle Charlie and her mother Irene on the adventure of their youth.

It's the last day of the nineteenth century and a massive theft, a sabotage of a cotton mill, has rocked their small town and put their livelihood and the livelihoods of so many others in danger. Charlie has his own ideas about who may be responsible. The police want him to leave it alone, but he can't do nothing while his family and neighbors may be kicked out of their homes.

The situation grows more dire when Charlie and Irene learn the mill has defaulted on its insurance payments. If they can't recover the stolen machinery, the mill will fold. And with it the whole town's economy.

Charlie and Irene race to find the mastermind behind the theft as the clock ticks closer to the new year. Will the century change be a marker of hope? Or will it be the end for their home?

Join the newsletter and get it now.

https://dl.bookfunnel.com/t63bwp5yny

Author's Note

Cora, Georgia is a made-up town full of made-up people, but there were some very real people who inspired this story. If you've had fun diving into the world of early 1920s airplanes and movie stars, these are some names to research further.

Jean Paige wasn't herself a pilot, but she was a famous actress in the 1910s and 1920s who had a reputation for doing her own stunts, some of which were quite dangerous. When I saw a photo of her character dangling from a rope out of an airplane, I knew I had to find a way to bring Hollywood glamour and barnstormer airshows together in this mystery and Agnes Lorraine's character was born.

While Bessie Coleman wasn't a direct inspiration for a character, during my research I was fascinated by her adventurous and trailblazing life…with a tragic ending. Bessie Coleman was the first African American woman and first Native American to hold a pilot's license. Because no one in the United States would teach her, she traveled to Paris to learn a few months after the events of this novel. She was known a daredevil flyer, attempting stunts others wouldn't dream of until she died in a plane crash in 1926.

Ruth Law was an early aviatrix who advocated for the United States to employ female pilots during World War I. They did not, but Ruth was a flight instructor who trained many male pilots fighting in the war. When I came across her in my research, I knew I needed to give Hank a female flight instructor as well.

About the Author

Connie B. Dowell writes mystery fiction and nonfiction for writers while her two kids climb all over her. When not writing, she podcasts, knits, plays violin badly, and binge watches Midsomer Murders. She lives in Virginia where she drinks far more coffee than is probably wise.

You can connect with me on:

🌐 http://conniebdowell.com
🐦 https://twitter.com/ConnieBDowell
📘 https://www.facebook.com/conniebdowellauthor

Also by Connie B. Dowell

Connie B. Dowell writes historical, modern, and paranormal cozy mysteries with kick-butt heroines and LGBTQ+ representation. Sometimes, the stories deal with tough issues in history and modern society, but all stories keep it sweet, no stronger than PG 13, and, of course, cozy.

The Poison in All of Us: An Emmie and Dessa Mystery (Book 1)
Christmas is supposed to be jolly fun. This Christmas season is murder.

In December 1918, college girl Emmie and her least favorite classmate, Dessa, are planning to enjoy the holidays, but their small town Georgia world is rocked when they find suffrage activist Miss Letty's murdered body. But that's not all…

Somebody's prowling around at midnight. Following Dessa.

And antisuffrage activists are getting louder and more aggressive.

Emmie and Dessa can't stand each other, but can they learn to work together and catch the killer before more women die? And will they do it before the bells ring on Christmas morning?

You'll love this short historical novel that's long on friendship and murder, because everyone's intrigued by a puzzling mystery.

Dead Man's Jazz: An Emmie and Dessa Mystery (Book 2)

Savannah, 1919: Two young ladies leave a speakeasy in the dead of night...

And walk right up to a murder scene.

Emmie and Dessa are on vacation, but their relaxing summer gets off to a dangerous start when they find a dead musician in a fountain. Then Theresa, Dessa's ex-girlfriend, is arrested for the crime. Dessa thinks she didn't do it, but the police are sure Theresa's the one.

Soon the girls are embroiled in a world of jazz, bootleggers, and activist groups with clashing goals, as they circle closer to the crime.

Meanwhile, the police find more evidence to pin on Theresa.

Can Emmie and Dessa find the killer before an innocent woman is hanged?

You'll love this book if you like twisty mysteries and the aesthetic of the early Jazz Age.

The Body in the Bookmobile: A Millie Monroe Mystery (Book 1)

Millie, a law school dropout, thinks she's landed a soft gig driving a bookmobile around the sleepy small towns of a mountainous Virginia county. But her first day on the job she finds a retired librarian dead in her van.

As the investigation continues and more bodies appear, the small town squabbles over things like an outdoor adventurer club or the proposed cell towers don't seem so innocent anymore. And the cops keep sniffing around the library. Could Millie's new friends and colleagues really be involved?

Surely not. There's no one more wholesome than librarians.

Right?

If you love twisty mysteries and a bisexual heroine with an unerring moral compass and a mean right hook, this is the book for you.

A Villain in the Vineyard: A Millie Monroe Mystery (Book 2)

It's the county's annual wine and beer festival. Bookmobile driver Millie is on hand representing the library system in a celebration of local brewing and winemaking history.

But when a body is found stabbed with a winery's corkscrew at a local brewpub's festival booth, the party's over. Could the killing have something to do with the rivalry between the two companies? Or is it all down to the wholesaler's shady past?

Tensions rise in the battle of wine versus beer. And Millie had better find the culprit before it's bottoms-up on another human life.

If you love twisty mysteries and a bisexual heroine with an unerring moral compass and a mean right hook, this is the book for you.

The Orchid Caper: Ian and Darlene (Book 1)

A down-on-her luck burglar, a trust fund college kid with something to prove. Will they outfox a master thief?

All eighteen-year-old Darlene wants is to rob the joint. College guy Ian comes home too soon. And some ill-timed flatulence brings them together. Darlene thinks she's toast. Instead Ian gives her a job offer, leading a heist team to steal a rare species of vanilla orchid. Only catch, she's swiping from one of the best thieves in the biz.

With her dad's store on its last legs, Darlene needs the cash she'll get when the job is done. Ian's in it to win a bet. Can their rag-tag team pinch the flower right under their mark's nose? And can they remember not to eat beans for breakfast?

The Orchid Caper is the first in a humorous YA action/adventure series. If you love action with a sense of humor, this is the book for you.

Death Among the Bluebells: A Garden Witch Mystery (Vella Serial Coming Soon)

Death Among the Bluebells: A Gard...
Connie B. Dowell

When Poppy's great aunt dies, leaving her a sprawling house and a friendly black and white cat, Poppy feels like she's won the jackpot... until she discovers her inheritance also includes the title of Resident Witch.

Just as Poppy's getting used to her new role, the small town is rocked by murder.

And newcomer Poppy is the number one suspect.

With her magic and the help of her new bestie and her lazy but powerful uncle, can she catch the real killer?

A Flock of an Alibi

A Flock of an Alibi, a flamingo themed cozy mystery anthology, from ten flocking good authors.

A Bird-Brained Scheme by Connie B. Dowell
   The Case of the Flamingo Fakery by S. Newell
   The Fatal Flamingo by Jemima Jenkins
   The Only Witness by Mary B. Barbee
   Red Herrings & Pink Flamingos by Brittany E. Brinegar
   Big Birds and Burglary by Rune Stroud
   The Biscuit Mix-Up by R. A. Muth
   Pink Flamingos and the Witch by J.J. Justice
   Azure and the Case of the Flocked Yards by Verena DeLuca
   Whole Lawn Of Love by Zoey Chase

www.ingramcontent.com/pod-product-compliance
Lightning Source LLC
Chambersburg PA
CBHW020425130626
46549CB00006B/2746